THE
SNAIL
KING

Previous Books by Charlie McFadden
The Picture Game
The Fiddlers Elbow
Stories From Around the Block

All available on Amazon

To Emily
My Sons James and Philip
And to the memory of a beautiful boy

All Characters are Fictional

Copyright © 2023 Charlie McFadden
All right Reserved
ISBN:

The Beginnings

If I were to tell you how a snail was once King or even Queen of the jungle, you'd probably laugh and think I'd gone bonkers, and most of the time you'd be right. But strange things happen more often than we realise, so here goes.

Most cultures, whether remote islands like Pitcairn in the Pacific Ocean or somewhere nearer to home, believe in God or a god of sorts. It's just one of those things, I don't know why; I guess no one does. That said, it stands to reason that this God or gods were present well before us, meaning humanity is just a chapter, not the whole book of life cover to cover.

Seneca Sigyn Seward was a god, she was beautiful, tall, with flowing red hair, lips of cherry and eyes an emerald green. As the God of Critique, it was her responsibility to weigh up the good and bad, which was a vital job as only through their understanding, do we grow stronger. That said, Seward Sigyn Seward was probably a little over keen in her work, pulling up all and sundry for any triviality, a ragged nail perhaps or a loincloth not quite covering the essentials, just trivial stuff. Her downfall came when she told Almighty Polypious, God of all Gods, that he needed to pull up his socks. The remark did not go down well.

Polypious' initial reaction was to demand that Seneca Sigyn Seward's eyes be plucked out, her face disfigured, and that she be bound over the Rock of Hesus to become a plaything for the gryphons. But Stodge, God of Chefs, who'd had his fair share of 'critique' from the overzealous Seneca Sigyn Seward, devised a better plan. *Why not cast her down to Earth, set her up as a King, and see how she copes with a bit of her own medicine?*

Polypious liked the sound of it and decided as a further measure that she would no longer be a thing of beauty; instead, Seneca Sigyn Seward would live as a lowly snail.

*

It may seem confusing that a female god is to become a King, but in this case, the word King should be viewed loosely, it could well be Queen. You may not know that snails are hermaphrodites, meaning they are both male and female; strange and quite fashionable these days, but snails don't care for fashion; it's just the way they are. There's always a sensible reason behind nature's dalliances, and here's why most gastropods are male and female. When looking for a mate, it doesn't matter to a snail who they meet on the slimy thoroughfare; after a quick introduction, they can get on and reproduce. Seems like a good idea to me, but what do I know?

And so it came to pass that Seneca Sigyn Seward, the God of Critique, was transformed into a humble snail, well an egg at first. She wasn't completely abandoned however, so when a hungry blackbird happened across a mess of snails' eggs, it gobbled to its heart's content but couldn't fit that last one in. And yes, you guessed it, Seneca Sigyn Seward hatched a few days later.

When she awoke, her flowing red hair and cherry lips were gone. Her once nimble grace, now a brown slug-like body with a heavy shell upon her back. On her head were beacon like tentacles with globes on the end, two for sight and two for smell.

Seneca Sigyn Seward yawned and blew out his/her snail cheeks. One of his/her eye stalks wandered forward whilst the other dawdled for a moment before pointing backwards as he/she took in her surroundings. He/she was...

Hold on a second, all this he/she, his/her business is already getting awkward, so from now on, I'll refer to Seneca Signy Seward simply by his/her name, and to make things even simpler still, I'll shorten it to just using Seward, and if at any time a name does not suffice, I will call Seward the Snail…. 'It'.

Seward's first days of life were unremarkable, with long hours eating and even longer hours snoozing, which might seem boring, but didn't bother Seward one bit.

You know, on second thoughts, 'It', isn't going to work, 'It', sounds clumsy and disrespectful for a former God, so from now on, let's say 'she' most of the time and if I slip up and occasionally say he, we can all live with it. A faff I know, but hey, let's get on with the story.

Seward had gobbled up the leaf she'd found herself on and so went off searching for some muscle-building flowers. Passing up on the reds, yellows, blues, and whites, she slowly made her way to a purple patch of pansies, which were to her taste.

Today, particularly in France, snails are considered a delicacy. There they gobble them down by the plateful, along with a glass or two of chardonnay. But the French are not the only ones who enjoy a snail slithering down the back of their throats. In fact, just about every living thing surrounding Seward was partial to one. With this in mind, Polypious assigned creatures to look out for her. So, when an absent-minded beetle ventured close to Seward, it received a very nasty nip from a dragonfly as a warning. When that same beetle returned for a second nibble, it got a sharp bite to boot. Slugs, ants, and worms all received the same treatment.

Seward quickly grew. Her eyes were now a curious green, her body a mottled mix of brown and orange hues, and her shell, a canopy of yellow with eight dark spiral bands. I'm not an expert on snails, but you'd be pushed to describe her as beautiful.

Now at the edge of the woodland, she paused and looked around. It was a shock. Everything seemed vast; the savanna, the sky, and the grazing animals appeared huge.

A crow landed and hopped over; its beady-eye winked at Seward, who smiled. The crow cawed, then grabbed her by the shell and was about to dash her onto the ground when something strange happened, something very, very strange indeed. With a crash, a colossal elephant called Plop burst out of the dense tree cover, running at full speed toward them. Panicked, the crow dropped Seward, flapped its wings and took to the air. Plop looked down at the little gastropod, picked her up and placed her on his back between his shoulders. With three loud trumpet blasts from Plop, eight of the tallest, strongest, biggest elephants you ever saw emerged from the trees. With trunks raised they approached, then bowed, which flabbergasted and confused little Seward. A sharp trumpet call from Plop and the herd moved off.

They had travelled for about half a day when it first started, a deep rumble, you know what I mean, a bit like an elephant's tummy playing up. The rumble got louder and louder and louder.

Peeping from her shell, Seward could see a huge black cloud in the distance and as they got closer, it became apparent that, in fact, it was not a cloud at all but a swarm of buzzing flies. The swarm were flying over a colossal herd of dusty wildebeest, going at breakneck speed towards the river.

Frightened, Seward crept as quickly as she could inside her shell. However, Plop and his companions had no such fear as they gazed at the spectacle. Plop raised his trunk and led the group forward at a trot. As if a siren had been sounded, the wildebeest screeched to a halt, staring at the gigantic pachyderms lumbering toward them. From his trunk, Plop blasted another call, then call after call, until a wide gap opened up in the herd. Wildebeest were bellowing in protest, some bucked and ran in panic, but most simply watched as the elephants trundled through, the leader with a tiny snail on its back. Once through, Plop rumbled out a softer melodious tone and the group steadied to a walk. Seward braved a peek, only to retreat as a massive grey trunk swung over to check on its load. Another trumpet blast, and they were on the move again.

Everybody knows that time is relevant; it's one of those things that's called a universal fact, Einstein or someone like Einstein said that. For humans, a day is 24 hours; 1440 minutes; or 86400 seconds. But time isn't always that simple. So, if I said a hundred years, you'd think that was a long time, a thousand years, well, that would be a very, very long time. But for this story, we've got to forget about all that. In this story, the Gods hadn't settled time; it could hop and skip forwards and backwards like a grasshopper from one leaf to the next before settling for a while, and then hopping to another. In those days time could just please itself.

For Seward, the journey took years; but for Plop and the other elephants, it was only days before they arrived at their destination.

The Palace of Xum

Plop gently tapped on Seward's shell.

In the distance were a row of jagged mountains that wrapped like a scarf around the Royal residence of the Animal Kingdom. It was very old, very big and very, very magnificent. The Palace of Xum was built way back, when Lily the Great, a rather gangly crocodile, established order in the Animal Kingdom.

The troop of elephants had now slowed to a steady walking pace. A still sleepy Seward looked up and could not believe her eyes. Tall marble walls with angular zigzag corners gave the Palace a majestic, if somewhat unusual appearance. Surrounding the Palace was a moat where lilies of every colour floated. Gibbon squeals and howls echoed through the air, announcing the arrival of the new King. The drawbridge dropped, the huge gate opened and four majestic giraffes emerged to greet them.

Seward's tiny snail heart fluttered in anticipation and wonder.

As General of the Guard, Plop led the procession through. The elephants marched together; each step punctuated with a drum beat.... boom.... boom.... boom. Cheers and whistles rose up from the gathered animals and creatures. From Aardvark to Zebra, all bowed or curtsied as Seward passed. As her eyes peered back and forth, it appeared as though Seward was waving. A huge cheer went up, some animals threw flowers, whilst others whistled and waved. Seward let out a tiny squeal of awe and delight. Well, who wouldn't?

A camel with a tall hat stepped forward and lifted Seward from Plop's shoulders, carefully setting her down onto a carpet of purple cabbage. Something guided the little snail, and after a very long time to some, but a speedy sprint for Seward, she reached the edge of a throne. A meerkat stepped forward carrying a tiny ramp, Seward slowly climbed up on it and at the top sat herself down on a cushion of silk and velvet. Two white unicorns stepped out from the crowd, their bodies adorned with stars, moons, and secret unicorn symbols. Trotting forward they curtsied in front of Seward, then split in opposite directions, meeting at a distant altar. Rearing up on their hind quarters, the unicorns performed a strange dance with their forelegs, it was as though they were casting a mysterious spell.

From her vantage point, Seward could now see that the altar was in fact a pyre on which lay the body of a dead lion, his golden mane gently moving on the breeze. To the side of it stood a raccoon, tall, straight back, bright inquisitive eyes, waxed whiskers, and a long-stripey tail, quite handsome in a rakish way. His name was Roly. As a trumpet peel rang out, he began reading from a scroll. He read verse after verse in praise of Polypious, God of all Gods. Roly's voice was clipped and as is often the case of those who have risen in rank, his vowels were somewhat overcooked. Once he'd finished, he bowed his head in silent prayer. A second trumpet peel rang out, Roly raised his eyes as from the skies ten white eagles appeared, each carrying a burning ember. In turn they swooped down dropping the smouldering cinders onto the pyre. Twenty stout elephants raised their trunks and blew until the embers fizzed into life, and then into a hungry furnace, with heat so intense that even the sturdiest turned away. As the flames consumed its prey all was silent, all witnesses solemnly bowed their head in respect of a king. When eventually the fire subsided, all that was left of the noble lion was ash.

Plop blasted a trumpet peel. A great white owl took to the air and, to stunned gasps, it dived into the centre of the embers and plucked out the smouldering heart of the lion. Rising up, it soared high into the sky, circled three times before swooping back down landing just in front of Seward. The owl hopped forward, tilted its head, paused a moment, blinked, then dropped the heart in front of her. As if on cue, Roly unfurled the scroll further and continued to read. Once finished, he bowed, and with the clumsy grace of an overly dramatic actor, threw himself prostrate in front of Seward. The assembled animals followed his lead. Even the snake representatives managed to press their scaly bellies lower than expected.

Seward gazed down at the lion's scorched heart, blackened with ash but still recognisable. Maybe it was a trick of the light, but it still seemed to be beating. Seward squealed in disgust, "Take it away."

No sooner had the words left her mouth when a huge vulture swooped, and the heart was no more.

Flower petals cascaded from upon high covering the grounds of the palace. One particularly juicy purple petal landed close to Seward, which reminded her that she had missed her lunch. She tentatively crept forward and took a bite, then another and another. Once finished, her eyes swivelled a full 360 degrees, she let out the tiniest of burps, which was only audible to herself, and then a little hiccup.

"Your Majesty, your subjects are waiting," said Roly, from his prone position.

"Waiting for what?" asked Seward.

Roly looked surprised, "Why, for your proclamation,

my lord."

The little snail took a deep breath and looked out at the crowds. All the animals were waiting in eager anticipation. *Proclamation, my Lord? What on Earth?*

From the side of his mouth, Roly whispered, "Your proclamation, my lord."

Seward wet her lips, "What?"

"Your subjects..." but before Roly had finished his sentence, Seward had retracted into her shell.

Unsure of what to do, Roly glanced up at Plop. Plop raised an eye, flapped his ears, shrugged, and looked to the great owl, who silently blinked an all-knowing eye.

Roly got to his feet and cleared his throat, "All noble representatives, worthy subjects. The King has advised me that the proclamation and coronation will now be conducted tomorrow."

From the multitude came a long drawn-out groan, which sounded like letting down a giant balloon, not quickly, but bit by bit. Some animals understood and dispersed immediately; but others, like the bumblebees and camels, were unsure, asking their neighbour what was going on.

Present among the crowd was someone that shouldn't have been there, someone with no royal blood or royal connections. Yes, you guessed right; it was a turkey. A black and brown turkey with white tail feather, a red wattle, and legs longer than you might expect. In truth he looked more like a dwarf Emu than a regular turkey. Ambitious, cunning and with designs on the crown, his name was Tommy Turkey.

It's a well-known fact that turkeys are sly, but Tommy Turkey was in a league of his own. Charming to your face, but as soon as you turned your back, you better look out. One of his favourite tricks was to pretend to be asleep, snoring like a good'un but listening all the time, just in the hope of overhearing a secret to use to his advantage. Like I said, sly, with a capital S.

As evening drifted into nighttime Tommy Turkey found himself a hide out to eavesdrop, one near the royal guests' quarters. From there he overheard the lizard prince saying he couldn't understand why the new King had not made a proclamation, "Not a good start, I'd say!" A slug representative of the mollusc family, suggested that Seward didn't look or even behave the part, "Far too ugly, and nervous to be our King." Tommy even heard a robin say she was partial to snails, laughing, "What could be tastier than a royal one."

Yes, Tommy Turkey's time had come.

*

Roly was dashing here and there, asking all sorts of questions of himself. *What if the King decides to nap tomorrow instead of delivering her proclamation? What if she hasn't prepared a proclamation speech at all? What if the proclamation concerned snails and how she planned to invite them onto the privy council? That would mean... Oh no, that would be disastrous. Oh no, oh no, oh no.*

Plop was standing guard over Seward. The unicorns, Harold and Berti, were brushing each other down, ensuring they looked beautiful and going over their routine for the following day's coronation event.

God of gods, Polypious was taking in a bit of sunshine on Mount Corrine, when Stodge, God of Chefs, turned up with a tasty cheese and onion flan.

"How's she getting on?" asked Stodge. "Any hissy fits?"

Polypious smiled, "Early days, early days."

The following morning our little snail awoke wondering about the previous day's events. *It had to have been a dream?* Seward chuckled. *It had to be. It just had to be.* She poked an eye out of her shell.

At this slightest movement, Plop trumpeted out such a

deafening note which shook and reverberated the whole Palace. Of course, it frightened the life out of Seward, who, in a flash, pulled back under cover.

There was a cough, another, then another. "Your Majesty," whispered Plop, he was holding out the tiniest silver tray you ever did see. On it was the sweetest strawberry you could ever imagine. On a scale of one to ten, it was about two hundred, almost as lovely as one of Harry's.

Now, you, the reader, don't know Harry, but take it from me, he was a young man with many good qualities, one being he grew the most beautiful, tasty strawberries.

Seward's sniffing tentacles peeked out from her shell, she could taste the sweet scent wafting back and forth. Slowly an eye emerged, then another.

Grinning, Plop moved the tray closer, "Your Majesty, your breakfast."

Harold and Berti were practicing their dance routine, it was a new one and was expected to be the highlight of the coronation event. Once finished they went inside to upset each other, as the fresh tears of unicorns were to be used to anoint the King.

In the meantime, Roly had taken the trouble to write up his own proclamation list, after hours of thinking and scratching, he stuck on seven.

They went something like this:

All animals and creatures must follow the guidance of their King.

All animals and creatures must follow the advice of the King's advisor.

All animals and creatures must respect one another.

All animals and creatures must avoid eating meat on Tuesdays.

All animals and creatures must avoid eating vegetables on Sundays.

All animals and creatures must not kill each other unless they have a good reason.

All animals and creatures must not forget to wash, particularly behind their ears.

*

When Seward looked up, Plop had a tiny napkin ready to wipe the strawberry juice from around her mouth.

"What day is it?"

"It's your coronation day, Your Majesty,"

"Yes, but what day?

Plop's eyes went to the sky as he calculated back from his birthday, which he knew was 205 days ago, and that was a Wednesday. As he counted, he'd nod as each day passed, pausing now and again to take a breath. Slowly he was getting there. He looked up and smiled, took another breath before going on.

It was obvious Seward was getting impatient, her one foot tapping with irritation.

Plop's eyes lit up; he was getting close. Then finally with his trunk punctuating his words, he counted down, "Tuesday, Wednesday, Thursday," he paused for a moment as though doubting himself before finally announcing, "It's Friday, Your Majesty."

Friday, I thought so." said Seward, letting out a wistful breath of annoyance. She shook her head, "Hmm, I think I need to go to the toilet."

Plop was shocked and a little embarrassed at the bluntness of Seward, but answered, "Oh, of course." He picked her up and carefully placed her down on her toilet, then politely turned and waited. After what he thought was a reasonable time for ablutions, he glanced back; Seward was finishing off and tidying herself.

Now, Tommy Turkey, despite his faults, was very diligent. He'd stayed up all night and was now perched on a mound overlooking Seward's quarters, making notes in his diary, *Snail wakes at 6.30am, breakfast - Strawberries.* To get a better view he craned his neck as far as it would go, but it was no good, he'd have to move. It was then that Plop noticed him, well not Tommy as such, but what looked like a black boulder walking very slowly across the courtyard.

Plop squinted against the early sunlight, *That can't be right*. He ducked a little and shaded his eyes. Yes, the boulder was moving. He took a few steps to the window, and realised it was not a boulder at all but Tommy Turkey creeping along, his body as close to the ground as to drag his feathers. "Excuse me for a moment, Your Majesty."

"What are you doing here?" Plop called out.

Pretending not to hear, Tommy Turkey took a hesitant step, then two more.

"What are you doing here?" repeated Plop, his voice raised. "You shouldn't be here."

"Oh, erm, err." The turkey's head slowly turned up to face the elephant. "Erm, erm, I was just on my way home," he glanced around and pulled a grin of confusion, "I... don't know how I've got here." Tommy chuckled, "Must of took a wrong turning." Despite his ugly turkey mug, he looked guiltless. He raised a wing to his eyes, then pointed, "I think I went... right, when I should have..."

"You should not be in here," Plop growled. "Only dignitaries, and you're not a dignitary."

"Oh really?" replied Tommy, he glanced up at the sun for some reason, "My fault, I could have sworn. ..." He was about to go on but seeing that Plop was lining up for what looked like a golf shot, quickly pulled in his head and legs.

With a swing of his trunk, Plop caught Tommy one hell of a clip, launching the unfortunate bird high into the air.

Flapping for all he was worth; Tommy flew over the Palace walls, squawking a painful gobble as he bounced once, twice three times, before sliding face-first into a boulder. He got to his feet, brushed himself down and rubbed his head, *That' it! They won't get away with this.* He huffed to himself, *I'll make Pippa the Python a proposal, one she's sure to accept.*

The Coronation

Seward was relaxing on her throne when Roly the Raccoon showed up to take her through his thoughts for the proclamation. Although they were well presented, and very neatly written, Seward quickly made up her mind that she did not like his ideas one bit, but she took her time to answer, "Washing and not eating on Sundays would not suit me." she coolly said and handed him back his notes. Seward didn't need some jumped up racoon to come up with her proclamation, she had ideas of her own. Excellent ones. She called for a pen and paper and something to lean on.

Roly rummaged around in his bag, "Your Majesty," he said, handing over a pen and scroll.

"And to lean on? said Seward irritated.

Roly smiled, turned his back and knelt on all fours.

Seward slithered forward, waited a moment, and then began to write.

Roly could feel the pen's pressure moving across his back and was trying to figure out what was being written. He was sure she started with a big O, then possibly an L or it could have been a P. Next, he felt two small i's, but then again, they could have been numbers, maybe two 1s.

Seward paused as though considering and let out a slimy huff before going on.

Roly felt zigzags and two sharp prods.

"There, I'm finished."

"May I look, Your Majesty?

"If you wish."

The scroll fell to the ground, Roly picked it up. It was all he could do to stop himself from bursting out laughing. In front of him was a badly drawn picture of a snail with a crown on its head. Roly looked to her, "Interesting, Your Majesty." Would… w…would there be any more… to add?"

Seward glared at him.

"No, no, of course! Very good, yes hmm, very good… yes."

"Away with you," Seward said, and with a sharp wave of a tentacled eye she dismissed him.

Roly went directly to the Dome of Wisdom; he needed to check on a few things, specifically, whether there was a precedent of a King's proclamation being challenged. Going over the records, he decided the only case relevant was that of Phileas the Zebra King, who had insisted in his proclamation that everything should be painted in stripes. His thought being that stripes made carnivores stand out, making the Kingdom of Xum a far safer place for herbivores.

Yes, absurd I know, but often absurdity and reality make good bedfellows and this was a good example.

The Zebra King's proclamation caused riots which then escalated into a civil war between the pro-stripes and anti-stripes. Many lost their lives, but after two years of bloody fighting, the carnivores had won. Despite the Zebra King losing the battle however, no one had the power to force him to abdicate. But a King without power is like a bird without feathers, exposed and pretty useless. After much diplomacy, the King had agreed to abdicate, but only on certain conditions. Firstly, as Zebras feared tigers the most, tigers had to keep their stripes, that was non-negotiable. Leopards and cheetahs, who at the time were honey-coloured, from then on would have spots. Now, the following condition is only known by a few people, so don't spread it around; it could get 'certain types' hot under their collars. Until then, female lions had magnificent manes like their lazy male counterparts. So, to give the herbivores fair warning of whether it was a ponderous male or a vigorous female in pursuit, female lions had to agree to give up their manes. Of course, the females, who were very fond of their luscious locks disagreed. But nevertheless, they were forced to yield. Phileas the Zebra King abdicated and a new Lobster Queen was crowned.

As Roly was gazing out the window, smiling to himself as he remembered the day he turned up at court, a young, scruffy orphan looking for shelter. It had been under the reign of Good King Gladys, the Peacock Queen. He was taken in, given a good scrub, and put to work under the Hedgehog Office Master. His first job was messenger deliverer, taking messages wherever required, but he soon progressed to message coordinator, which meant he would take messages wherever required and also return them to the Hedgehog Office Master. As the years passed Roly had made his way up the ladder to a place of power and now was the official Kings Advisor. He considered himself good and honest and had always done his best for those he'd served. It was just that Seward didn't strike Roly as King material; perhaps it was too much responsibility for someone so inexperienced? He pondered on the naivety of how she'd dismissed his proclamation list out of hand, not even giving it a second reading. Roly shook his head; he certainly did not want to cause friction, but…

The sun was tip-toeing towards its zenith, time was

ticking on. A chorus had started outside the Palace, initially by the hyenas and howler monkeys, but soon all the animals joined in, with the elephants trumpeting an accompaniment.

Roly let out a huff; it wasn't personal, *Stupid animals*. He'd better get ready.

"God save our gracious King

God save our noble Queen…

He is our Queen

God save our noble King

God save our gracious Queen…

She is our King"

As the sound lifted, Seward was drawn to the window of her Royal quarters. "Is that for me?"

Plop nodded, "Yes, Your Majesty."

Seward felt flattered. Stretching as high as she could, she waved down with her tiny tentacled eyes.

A huge cheer went up, "Hip-hip-hooray! Hip-hip-hooray! Hip-hip-hooray!"

Plop called for six of the stoutest elephants to join him, and proceeded to make his way to the Palace gates. The masses were being divided into two orderly lines, one going to the left and the other to the right. There was a bit of jostling, particularly from the crocodile and crab contingents, but eventually all managed to filter in and find a place to settle.

At twelve noon exactly a gongs tone fluttering over the Palace walls and off into the distance, bong, bong. The animals settled their chatter and a hush descended as the gong sounded again.

Harold and Berti, the unicorns, stepped out into the courtyard, gowns flowing and tails held high.

A huge cheer went up.

Directly behind them were two rows of peacocks, their colourful feathers shimmering in the breeze. They were followed by twenty lions partnered with twenty buffalos, 'lesser' Kings and Queens in their own right. Then pairs of rhinos, bears and chickens. The final column was a single line of fifty tortoises. On the final tortoise sat Seward, dressed in a gown of purple and gold with a train of iridescent silk. She waved graciously as the crowds threw flowers. The sight was awe-inspiring.

A trumpet sounded sharp and true, a signal for the monkey minister who stepped forward and gently lifted Seward onto her throne. There she sat, as dignitaries of the Kingdom in turn bowed before her.

With each slow step, Roly's paw slid forward, like some type of shuffle. Once in position, he unfurled the scroll he was holding and began reading, "On the authority bestowed on me…." It was a long speech which droned on and on. Some animals began chatting to one another. Roly could hear the moans, but he wasn't cutting short his speech for anyone. After all, this was the coronation of a new King, not some baby getting its head wet. *No, groan as much as you want.* Such an occasion required ceremonial gravitas.

Whistles went up and the occasional boo. Even Seward become so bored that she had become distracted by a bee buzzing overhead.

Finally, Roly came to an end of his speech, then bowed to Seward.

Harold and Bertie stepped forward and together they curtsied, their horns gently touching Seward. Harold went to one side of the throne, Bertie to the other. It was back to Roly again; in his paws he held a chalice filled with unicorn tears, which he held aloft. Once more the exaggerated steps moved across the stage. He bowed, then dipped a paw into the chalice and carefully anointed the new King.

From faraway came the haunting tones of one hundred whales. They were joined by the song of a thousand blackbirds. This was the signal for the final act, Seward was to be crowned. A silver beetle shuffled across the stage, on its back was a tiny velvet cushion on which was placed Seward's crown.

Roly picked up the crown, held it aloft. It was made from the shells of Jewel Beetles, sparkling iridescent shades of green. Roly bowed and carefully placed it on Seward's head.

As a cheer went up, more flower petals fell from the sky.

Seward held her head high, then turned to the left, the centre, and the right.

Plop nodded an instruction and two meerkats scurried off, returning moments later carrying what looked like a megaphone made from a rubber plant leaf, placing it down before the King.

Seward was a little non-plussed, then remembered. "Oh yes." Speaking as loudly as a tiny snail could, she began, "My proclamation today." She then raised her voice, "My proclamation is for everyone to get a little bit tiddly."

There were laughs and the odd chuckle from the audience. Most thought it was a joke or they'd misheard. Roly looked astounded.

Seward rolled her eyes dismissively, leant forward and repeated, "Everyone to get a little bit tiddly."

Although he too was confused, Plop spoke in a deep baritone, "Everyone to get a little bit tiddly."

The chuckles and guffaws turned into howls of laughter; the hyenas were on their backs, chimpanzees too.

Seward looked perplexed, she turned to Plop, raised a commanding eyebrow, "We have sufficient nectar in the cellars I hope?"

Plop thought for a moment. It was well known that the golden nectar had magical powers and was only ever served to Kings and Queens, and only then on very rare occasions. It had never… in his lifetime, been served up to ordinary jungle animals. He had his concerns, his lips fumbled but he made no sound.

Seward fixed him with an icy stare.

His words arrived in flutters and stutters, "Yes…

yes... my Lord." He called to the servants, "To the cellars, bring up the nectar."

They funnelled off, returning minutes later with two large wooden barrels of the golden liquid. The chief meerkat lifted off the lids whilst her minions scooped out bowlfuls of nectar, handing them to the pelican waiters.

Initially most were unsure, the odd lap from the cats, a cautious finger from the apes, even the usually greedy seagulls seemed hesitant. Soon, however, nectar was being gulped and guzzled down by the gallon. The delicious magical liquid had a strange effect, savage wolves began playing with lambs, eagles gave rides to ducklings, and mice were tickling and laughing with crocodiles. But soon scuffles broke out, a moose picked a fight with a grasshopper, and then a few of the camels took offence to a remark by a caterpillar. Plop sent in some elephants into the crowd to make sure the fights were quelled with no severe injuries. Bizarrely, as quickly as the quarrels arose, everyone became friends again. Very strange indeed. Seeing what was happening, Plop commanded his guards to abstain and remain alert.

"All hail the King," the animals called out in slack unison, "All hail King Seward."

A grinning Seward watched on, she took a sip of

nectar herself, "Look Plop, they're enjoying it. I knew it would work."

Plop let out a low rumble.

Feeling energised, "I think I'm going to make another proclamation." Seward's head went to one side as she considered. Plop's nervousness caught her eye, she giggled, "But maybe not today."

In the crowd, Tommy Turkey had been making notes. He particularly noticed the shock on Roly's, and that the raccoon had refused the nectar. The turkey grinned and nudged Pippa the Python, "Did you see that?"

The Python flicked out her tongue and hissed.

*

"Haven't I done well for my first day? I think it's been a great day," said Seward as Plop tucked her in for the night.

"Yes, Your Majesty, everyone enjoyed it.

"They did, didn't they?" Seward laughed, adding pensively, "My reign will be a joyful one, I think." She yawned. "It's been marvellous." Her head craned to the thimble of nectar by her bedside, "Just one more sip. Oh, and another," she giggled. "Oops," as she knocked the nectar onto the floor. "Never mind, no harm done. I'm tired now, and must get my beauty sleep. Thank you and good night, Plop."

"Good night, Your Majesty," replied Plop as he quietly tiptoed from the Royal Quarters.

Nectar

It was early the following day; the sun was barely out of its pyjamas when all were woken by a banging and crashing. Someone or something was battering the Palace gates. Gibbon sentries were squealing, throwing sticks and coconut shells down from the battlements.

Plop swung his head and shouted, "What in heavens?" as he marched over to the heavy gates. He slid open the spy hole, and had barely his eye in place when the gate violently rocked back into his face. Letting out a painful squeal, Plop shouted, "What's going on out there?" Things went quiet for a moment. He leant forward for another peek, just in time to see a rhino pawing the ground, ready for a relaunch. Fearful of getting another nasty bash, Plop pulled his face away.

Bang, as the rhino hit the gates again.

The chief look-out swung down onto the elephants back and lifted Plop's ear. "Nectar! nectar!"

Although a little concussed, Plop pointed to a half-filled barrel of leftovers, "Give it that and tell it to calm down. The King is asleep and won't take too kindly to being woken."

In seconds, four gibbons jumped from their posts and hauled the barrel forward.

"Get a move on," called Plop.

As soon as the gates opened, the rhino thundered forward, scattering the skittish gibbons and with a swing of its head sent the barrel high into the air, spinning three times before crashing to the ground. The crazed animal galloped over, let out a loud snuffling noise, shoved its face into the sand and began lapping at the golden nectar.

A flurry of gibbons dashed forward to share in the feast, but the bad-tempered rhino didn't take kindly to sharing. But no sooner had the rhino frightened one gibbon away, than another greedy hand dipped into the delicious liquid.

Plop came thundering forward, his trunk raised in alarm, "What's going on?"

The rhino glanced up, mouth filled with sand and nectar and grunted a warning. Raising himself to his full height, Plop blasted out his own warning. He wasn't going to take any nonsense from a rhino. He scooped up a cloud of dust and flung it into the air, and followed with a threatening charge. But the rhino wasn't intimidated. Letting out a dismissive grunt, it dug its horn into the ground and flicked a wave of sand into the air.

Plop had never seen this behaviour from any of the rhinos, well maybe a crazy adult male, but this rhino was small, probably a female. He trumpeted another warning, swung his trunk and blustered forward. It was then he spotted in the distance two rhinos galloping towards them. Now one rhino he could handle, but three would be a handful, so he called for help.

The rhinos arrived out of breath, explaining that it was their daughter who was causing all the trouble. Mother Rhino said she was usually a very good girl, but that nectar had caused her to act strangely, so much so they had struggled to get her home the previous evening. Mother Rhino took a deep breath, saying an antelope had woken them to tell them about the commotion at the Palace, and they'd dashed over as quickly as they could. The father rhino snorted, suggesting it was irresponsible of the King to give out nectar in such a loose fashion, "Jungle animals are not used to it," he objected.

Plop pondered as the rhinos escorted their daughter away; *maybe, they were right. He, too had concerns about Seward's proclamation.* He dipped his trunk into the nectar barrel and tasted some. Just regular sweet nectar, but the gibbons were back, screaming and fighting for the dregs.

Exploring

Seward called for Plop; and a servant scampered off. A few minutes later she could hear his heavy footsteps. As he entered her rooms, she smiled, "I would like a tour of the Palace."

Plop scratched his head, "As you wish, Your Majesty."

Plop picked her up and placed her gently in the middle of his shoulders.

"Giddy up," said Seward.

From the courtyard gardens, they toured the bedrooms, the library, bathrooms, ballroom and the kitchen areas. None were of interest to Seward, so she urged Plop on. Next went to the Throne Room, which again held little appeal for the King.

"Stop! Stop!" Seward commanded.

They were in the Long Gallery. On its wall were portraits of previous Kings and Queens, mostly lions, but with a fair smattering of zebras, rhinoceros, a couple of elephants, an ostrich, and a praying mantis.

"Who are you?" asked Seward spotting a three-toed sloth dressed in an artist's smock, paintbrush at the ready.

"I'm Sammy." The sloth smiled.

"And what are you doing Sammy?"

"Oh, oh, I'm working on a portrait of the Lion King Scampi, Your Majesty."

"Hmm," Seward slithered forward to look over Sammy's shoulder. The Lion King was looking directly out from the painting; regal, if somewhat severe. "Can you do one of me?" Seward asked, but then changed her mind, "No, wait, get me some paint and some paper," she commanded.

"Ye…s Your…ur..Maj..esty," said Sammy, reaching very, very slowly for the materials.

Talk about a snail's pace, Seward shook her head in frustration, huffed, then looked up at Plop, "We'll be here all day, you get it for me."

The elephant's trunk swung forward almost knocking the poor sloth off its stool. He picked up a selection of paints and paper and gave them to Seward.

Seward certainly had a unique painting style, best described as dynamic and vigorous. Splashes went this way, splashes went that way, and some paint went on the paper.

"There... I'm finished."

Plop reached over for the painting.

"Well, what do you think?" asked Seward proudly.

Plop couldn't make it out, to him it was just a mess of colour. He held it as far away as possible and refocussed, turned the painting one way, then another. Yes, he'd got it now. It was a very poorly painted picture of a snail wearing a long purple ballgown, a tiara and with long dangly earrings.

"I practised this morning," Seward announced, "Pretty good, eh?"

Plop blinked and blinked again. "It certainly has energy, Your Majesty. It's er... more than good, it's perfect. Yes, perfect, perfect."

"And you there," Seward looked down at Sammy.

The sloth smiled.

"I thought so. How many kings before me have been excellent artists?" Without waiting for the sloth to respond, "Put it up over there," Seward commanded, pointing to a space that had been reserved for Lion

King Scampi. "Gluepot."

The glue smelt disgusting, Plop reluctantly dipped the end of his trunk into it and pasted the picture onto the wall.

"Onwards, onwards!" ordered Seward, giving Plop a sharp tap on his head. As they were leaving, she turned to look back to admire her handywork and grinned to herself.

Next on the agenda were the royal pleasure gardens where they strolled amongst the wildflowers, trees and shrubs. It was a treat for the eyes and Plop's favourite place to spend an afternoon; the aroma was magnificent. Even as he carried his King, he couldn't help but swing his trunk back and forth, taking in every microscopic sweet scent on offer.

"Can you just pick for me… that pansy?" said Seward pointing to a purple one.

*

Seward was sitting up in bed, breakfasting on a strawberry, "Where did this come from? It's not to my liking," said Seward, spitting it out. "So, my Kingdom?"

"Which Land would you want to visit first, Your Majesty?"

"Which of my Lands? What do you mean?"

"Which of your Lands?" Plop repeated. "Xum is divided, Your Majesty. We have Aqua Land, Reptilian Land, Bird Land, Insect Land and Mammalian Land.

Looking confused, Seward slumped forward, "My subjects are divided?"

"Yes, Your Majesty."

"Why?"

Plop explained, "Five hundred years ago, during the reign of Aloysius the King it was split."

"What in heavens for?" said Seward, waiting for an explanation.

"Before we became civilised, some animals mixed," said Plop raising an eyebrow.

Seward waved for him to continue. "Yes… Yes!"

Plop took a deep breath, "Which resulted in the epoch of Unheavenly Creatures."

Seward seemed astonished.

"Yes, Your Majesty, monstrosities! Dogs with the heads of swans, flying cats, pigs with wings…

dolphins procreated with eels, their offspring beasts with a head at both ends. Horses with insect legs that could outrun the wind itself."

Flabbergasted, Seward replied, "How strange… A dog with a swan's head, dolphins with two heads and horses…?"

"Yes, and many more my Lord?" replied Plop.

"Where can I see these wonderous creatures?" said Seward gleefully.

"Nowhere, my Lord. Thankfully, none exist today, but there are drawings."

*

In the library, Plop picked up a large heavy book, blew off the dust and laid it on a table. The cover was tatty in the extreme, but the insides were immaculate. Gold letters on the first page read, ***The Book of Unheavenly Creatures***.

Seward looked on as Plop turned the first page. They were met by a magnificent drawing of a monstrous freak of nature. In colours of purples, greens, and orange was a caterpillar with the legs of a frog and the tail of a serpent. Plop turned another page. This time they were met with what looked like a goose, but with the head of a donkey and the wings of an insect.

Another page, then another, each animal stranger than the previous.

They were halfway through the book when Seward asked Plop to stop. She was thinking things over. After a few moments of contemplation, "Another page, please."

Next was a bestial creature with a fish's head, zebra's legs, a worm's body with a snail's shell, and a single wing.

Seward grimaced, "And the next one, please."

This time it was a rhino with the legs of an ostrich, a peacock's tail and a set of thorny antlers protruding from its head.

Seward shook her little head, "Plop... Plop, do you believe these creatures actually existed?"

Plop flicked the last page back and forth, "Of course, Your Majesty, they're here in the book." He turned to the front cover and read out loud the title, *The Book of Unheavenly Creatures.*

Seward looked at him, "Hmm... "And who exactly created this book?

Plop's eyes drifted to the ceiling, once again his mind working back from some memorable event. "I think..." He tapped the side of his head with his trunk, "Come on now." He let out a grunt, "Yes, yes... got it, got it.... It was ..."

Seward smiled, a hint of sarcasm in her response, "Did Great King Aloysius do anything else?"

"He built this wonderful Palace!" said Plop.

Looking around at the magnificent structure, Seward couldn't fail to be impressed, but something was bothering her.... "I think I may make another proclamation once I have seen the whole of my Kingdom."

*

Touring a Kingdom cannot be done quickly, especially if you are a snail. For Seward, it took five years, four months, one day and twenty-one seconds. For Plop, a week and a half.

As she travelled, Seward was struck by the variety of animals under her care. It made her mind boggle. From huge whales to tiny insects. As the King, wherever she went she was feted and besieged with requests. One, I recall was in Insect Land. At that time, butterflies were like their duller cousins the moths, plain brown and buff. But while moths were workmanlike and dour, butterflies loved dancing and partying. Their request was, *"Brighter colours."*

On seeing how they flitted so joyfully, Seward readily agreed, "Any colour you like," she announced, and without a second thought, butterflies became the wonderous array we see today. Another was in Aqua Land, where salmon asked if they could leave the rivers where they'd been born. With a wave of a tentacle, Seward gave them the freedom of the vast oceans, but on the condition that they return to the rivers and streams of their birth, to make love and multiply. In Mammalian land it was that old chestnut. They all wanted more to eat. Seward put on her thinking cap and quickly came up with the solution. Vegetarians should try meat now and again, and as for carnivores, well why not give vegetables a go. Dogs, apes, pigs, etc, thought it a great idea and went with it. But no matter how hard she tried to change the minds, of eagles, crocodiles, bears and quite a few others, they stubbornly refused to change. Tigers in particular made a fuss, saying greens upset their stomachs, which seemed nonsense to Seward. In the end, the King lost her patience, saying they'd have to sort it out themselves.

In Reptilian Land. Seward hoped that the long-lived beasts would provide some answers on the question of unheavenly creatures. But no sooner had she arrived there when she was faced with a complex puzzle.

Two gecko mothers were fighting each other, hissing,

spitting, and biting. The action was fierce.

Tired after her long journey Seward was in no mood for their antics. She stamped her foot and shouted, "Quiet!" At once the two geckos stopped. Seward commanded them to approach.

Each gecko held a baby, one child was alive, the other dead. The mother holding the dead baby was in tears and claimed the other gecko had stolen her baby. The other grinned, swiped her tail, hissing and spitting at the distraught mother. In a flash they set at each other again.

"Separate them!" cried Seward, as Plop intervened. Seward had her suspicions who was telling the truth and who was lying and also knew a decision was required. After a few moments pondering, Seward came up with a solution. The living baby lizard was to be divided; one mother to have the front end and the other the tail. A sharp-toothed crocodile was called forward, and the living child was placed in its jaws. Seward thoughts were that the gecko most upset at the idea, would be the true mother. But things didn't go that way. No sooner was the baby in the crocodile's mouth, than the jaws snapped shut, slicing the little fella in two, resulting in two dead ends.

One mother broke down, tears flowing down her scaly cheeks. Whilst the other found the whole thing amusing, laughing to her heart's content. Seward felt dreadful, but what could she do?

Polypious, God of all Gods was peering down over the edge of a cloud, he chuckled. A wail came from Angela, God of Mothers, who pleaded for the life of the baby gecko. Being very fond of Angela, Polypious waved his hand and time stood still as they debated the issue. Finally, Polypious relented, he took a deep breath and blew, and as he did tiny sparks fell from the sky over the lifeless body. Miraculously both ends of the baby gecko twitched three times, then jerked back to life.

No one was more surprised than Seward, who proclaimed that the truthful mother should have the front end and the mother who lied was left with the tail, which died soon after. From that day in Lizard Land, tails were known as liars.

Word soon spread that the King was able to challenge nature. Wherever she went animals trailed, some wanting healing, some a blessing, and some simply to see the snail who could work miracles.

*

Their last stop on the Royal Tour was Bird Land

Getting everything ready, Plop had rounded up a caravan of fifty camels, twenty donkeys, fourteen reindeer. "Your Majesty," he said, inviting Seward forward.

When unsure, Seward would blink each eye separately, once, twice, and then a third time, not fast blinks but slow considering blinks, and only then would she make up her mind. "I'm not sure I want to travel today; perhaps we should spend another day here. Yes, let's stay here. Maybe tomorrow."

The cortège was stunned in disbelieve, many grumbled but no one said a word.

Tomorrow arrived at five o'clock on Tuesdays. Seward was up early, and after a juicy strawberry for breakfast, she was raring to go. "Onwards to Bird Land."

Plop re-organised the caravan of fifty camels, twenty donkeys and fourteen reindeer and once satisfied that all were present and correct, he let out a trumpet blast.

As the caravan moved though the lush jungle of Bird Land, Seward was delighted. It was an absolute feast for the eyes. Birds of greens, blues, yellows, and every combination of colour one could imagine were there, and then there was song.

Bird central was a hive of activity when they arrived. Young chicks were running about playing, love birds were courting, older birds were perched, chirping over the day's events. Seward liked Bird Land; it was the sort of place a snail could feel comfortable. She soon noticed that there seemed to be some sort of strata, or hierarchy. On the ground were a flock of dodos, along with a mass of pigeons, in the lower tree branches were jungle fowl, next step up were parrots and peacocks, higher up still were bigger birds, eagles, storks and at the very top of the canopy were the albatrosses.

On spotting the cortege, Tommy Turkey trotted over. Lowering a wing, he bowed graciously, "Welcome Your Majesty, what a pleasure." *Could it be a simple visit? Maybe the King has heard of my skills and assets and wants me in her court? Or, heavens forbid, what if Pippa the Python has grassed me up?*

Plop raised his trunk, "All hail the King," his voice a rumbling timbre as he placed Seward onto the jungle floor.

The response was a chorus of clucks and shrills. A giant red cockerel leant back and let off three rounds of a cock-a-doodle-doo. Plop stretched out his trunk and bugled out a trumpet call of his own.

At that there was a crashing sound of twigs and branches. A flustered looking ostrich appeared through a thicket of vegetation. It was Madame Ostrich, Chief Bird of Bird Land Council. "Your

Majesty, you are most welcome." Her nervousness was plain to see as she skipped back and forth, her big feet all the time getting closer and closer to where Seward had been set down. Plop swung out his trunk and gave her a gentle slap, which seemed to bring her to her senses.

Madame Ostrich stamped her giant foot and with a strange gurgle from her throat she sent a young magpie off to find something for the King to eat.

The magpie returned a few moments later with some lettuce in its beak.

Madame Ostrich graciously bowed her head and smiled.

Seward looked at the limp offering, quickly dismissing it with a, "No, thank you." She looked to Plop, "Could you kindly bring me The Book of Unheavenly Creatures, please."

Without instruction, four meercats dashed off, returning moments later carrying the heavy book.

"Can you kindly request Madame Ostrich to view please," said Seward.

The book was placed upon a rug. Madame Ostrich approached, followed by a stork peering over her shoulder.

Plop turned the first page, which showed an animal with four heads and five tails. Madame Ostrich looked bewildered. Plop turned the next page, on which was a creature with a beetle's body, the head of a worm, feathered wings, and a fluffy rabbit's tail. Plop turned another page.

Page after page was inspected until Seward addressed the ostrich. "You are familiar with these beasts, no doubt?"

With eyelashes dancing like caterpillars on a swing, Madame Ostrich looked down at the book, then to her King, then to the book again, and once more to the King, "Your Majesty, I am but a simple bird. These creatures are beyond my knowledge."

"You are sure?"

Madame Ostrich nodded and glanced around, "Fellow birds, have any of you seen these strange creatures?"

There was the sound of flapping of wings, a squawk or two, and soon flocks of inquisitive birds were on the ground, all of them inspecting the book.

A voice rang out, "Gobble…gobble…gobble." It was Tommy Turkey flapping for all his worth as he pushed to the front.

Plop stuck out his trunk, stopping the turkey in his

tracks.

"Your Majesty, please let me present myself," said the turkey.

"Let him approach," said Seward.

Tommy Turkey smiled.

Plop frisked the turkey, just in case he was carrying a weapon, then looked to Seward, who nodded.

"Tommy Turkey at your service, Your Majesty." He bowed, "Yes, Your Majesty, I know of such creatures." He was, of course, lying. "My great, great, great, great, great, great grandfather told me about them."

Seward was no fool, her eyes raised, keenly examining the tricky rapscallion, "Your great, great, great, great, great, great grandfather told you?"

"Yes."

"How old is he?" Seward asked.

"Gibbledy gobbledy goop," said Tommy Turkey. *Which in human language meant eight hundred and twelve years old. I know that sounds a lot, but please remember that at the time of this story, time had not yet settled.*

"Where is he? I want to meet him," said Seward nonchalantly.

Tommy Turkey lowered his head, placing a wing over his heart, "He is not with us, Your Majesty."

Seward looked past Tommy, "Fetch him! Does he not know his King is present?"

"Alas, he has joined his ancestors and the Gods," Tommy Turkey replied, glancing up at the heavens.

There was a moment of puzzlement, then a faint flicker of a memory, but before Seward could gather it, the memory was gone, "Oh, I see… Anyway, you know of such creatures?"

Tommy Turkey scratched the ground, a sure sign he was about to tell a lie. "Yes, they are said to live on the outer edges of the Kingdom. When I was a chick, I was taken there."

"You saw them?"

Tommy Turkey scratched the ground again…. another lie, "In abundance, Your Majesty."

"In abundance, you say?" With a wave of her tentacle Seward signalled for Plop. In the tiniest of whispers that only an elephant could hear, she asked, "What do you make of this turkey? Does he speak the truth?"

Plop covered the little snail with his ear and whispered something that only they shared.

Seward was about to reply when there came a shout. "Liar, liar, your pants are on fire," it was from one of the parrots.

Tommy Turkey spun around, spoiling for a fight, "Who said that?"

To howls of laughter, the parrot repeated the claim, not once or twice but three times.

"Come down here and say that," said Tommy boastfully. "Hmm…hmm, yeah, thought so. A chicken with a loud mouth and nothing to back it up!"

At that the parrot took to the air and disappeared into the jungle.

Tommy returned his attention to the King. "Your Majesty, if you allow me, I can take you to where these creatures live." He waited a moment, "I could take you now?"

Of course, he had no intention of taking Seward to the edge of the Kingdom, his plan was to isolate her from Plop…. And if he managed that, it was curtains for the royal snail and the beginning of the Turkey dynasty.

"Take his details," said Seward with a flamboyant wave of a tentacle, "We'll be in touch."

Tommy Turkey eagerly handed over his business card, a small slip of parchment with a crude drawing of himself. Plop accepted the card and slipped it behind his ear.

Tommy bowed and clicked his heels, "Forever at your service, Your Majesty."

Seward nodded and watched as the turkey trotted off. *What a strange funny fellow.*

Plop frowned, eyebrows creasing in concern. "Your Majesty, I advise utmost caution."

Seward nodded, "You are right, we must approach this with care. Let us gather more information." But the turkey had made an impression and his words played on her mind.

As bedtime approached, Seward settled down for the night, and as she dozed, her thoughts went to The Book of Unheavenly Creatures. The idea that extraordinary creatures once existed stirred in her a mix of fascination and apprehension. Perhaps there was some truth to the legends and tales. Through sleepy eyes, she looked up, "Plop, do you believe those strange creatures existed?"

Plop pondered the question, but only for a moment, "Of course, why else do we have such books, if not to warn us."

When you least expect it

The Royal Caravan had left Bird Land, and were on their way home.

Plop was leading and was about fifty yards in front of everyone else. As he looked off into the distance, he could just make out the outline of the Palace. Something didn't seem quite right, he pushed on, but after another mile or so, he halted.

"What's going on?" asked Seward of one of the servants.

"I don't know, Your Majesty."

Plop raised his trunk and sniffed the air. Taking few more steps he could see it now. A large animal was chasing around in front of the Palace causing havoc. He recognised the beast; it was the rhino who had caused all the fuss previously. He waved for two guards to join him and together they charged forward and surrounded the rhino.

The rhino bucked and swung her head, but could not break free. "Nectar! Nectar!" she called out as she was dragged forward.

Once inside the Palace, Plop looked around and

couldn't believe his eyes. The portcullis was on the ground, the drawbridge down, and solid walls now merely piles of rubble.

A terrified looking Roly the Raccoon appeared at the entrance to his quarters. "She's gone crazy! Crazy! I tell you! She's wrecked everything. Look what she's done, carnage! carnage!"

With a moment's distraction, the rhino broke free and seemed determined to get to Roly.

The nimble footed racoon jumped onto Plop's broad back. "What did I tell you, crazy!"

With Plop pushing from the rear and elephants either side, the deranged rhino was escorted through the Palace grounds. Lifeless bodies were strewn everywhere, a mutilated giraffe, its neck twisted a funny angle, twenty or more dead gibbons, and the corpses of at least fifty meerkats. Surviving servants were either crying, others simply staring in shock.

No one remembered when the stockade was last used; it had been built during the war, which no one could remember. With heavy tree trunks as walls, it was the only place secure enough to hold a rampaging rhino.

Once released, the heavyweight herbivore ran full throttle testing the barrier. Crash, bang! In her delusional state, the tree trunks laughed at her, "Is that all you've got?" The rhino snorted and charged at the other side, but they too, mocked, "Call that a charge?" Now she was running at anything, a water trough, a boulder, straw, hay, even dust on the ground, each leaving her with a scornful remark. This went on for hours until eventually her mania subsided and exhausted she slumped to the ground. Only then did Plop call forward the Royal Caravan.

As she entered the Palace, Seward snapped into her shell, calling out from inside, "What's happened?"

Roly shook his head, sarcastically repeating, "What has happened?"

"Your Majesty, we need to make sure you are safe." Plop called for one of the guards to escort Seward to her quarters.

In the courtyard, Plop buttonholed Roly, "What happened?"

The raccoon explained that after they had left to tour the Kingdom, the rhino had returned looking for nectar. On the first day she rampaged through the cellars. The day after that she raged through the rest of the Palace. Again and again, she continued her orgy of destruction. Any creature in her way was trampled or skewered by her enormous horn. Roly was so fearful he'd locked himself in his quarters.

"And how long has this been going on?"

"Since you left."

Plop sent for the rhino's parents. They arrived later that day, and against Plop's better judgement, he took them to the stockade.

On seeing their daughter Mother Rhino cried, father too.

"Bring her forward," called Plop.

Two elephants dragged the exhausted rhino towards the side, a huge rope confining her movement. She didn't look well. Her eyes were absent and bloodshot, and her ribs stuck out from her sides like a bony cage.

Father and Mother Rhino looked her and then at each other, they knew the sentence for killing any creature in the Palace of Xum was death, never mind this genocide.

Mother Rhino spoke, "Can you speak to the King? Can you ask for clemency?"

Plop was resolute, "The Book of Justice is quite clear that punishment is death. No exceptions."

The young rhino gazed vacantly at her parents, "Nectar! Nectar! Give me nectar!"

Plop glanced at the gawking gibbons, "Is there any left?" One dashed away, returning with a small bowl of the golden liquid.

The caged rhino's eyes lit up. "Please. Please."

Seward was watching the proceedings from her balcony. *What on Earth could have happened? Had there been some explosion or maybe an earthquake?* There was a knock on the door, "Enter!"

A young meerkat presented a silver tray of strawberries and flower petals, and without saying a word put the tray down. He bowed and turned to leave.

"I say, you there! What has happened? Has there been an earthquake?"

The meerkat seemed unsure as to whether she was allowed to speak.

"I command you, tell me!"

The servant relayed the tragic events.

*

When Plop arrived at the Kings quarters, he looked tired and agitated.

"What's going on down there?"

"The rhino is being held, Your Majesty. I am making arrangements for the execution. I need you to sign the warrant." Plop held out a scroll, his trunk was shaking.

Seward began reading.

'Whoever shall be guilty of conducting death within the Palace of Xum shall be deemed a royal heretic. The punishment for such an act is death by tickling. The tickling to be conducted before the cock crows on the morning following the act.'

Now tickling may not seem to be an efficient method of execution, but efficiency was not what The Book of Justice had in mind. Tickling was the slowest and cruellest method of execution, not a fun experience at all.

Seward read over the warrant again and again. Finally, "Plop, take me to the rhino. I want to speak to her."

"It is too dangerous, Your Majesty. It would be unwise."

"Fiddlesticks. You'll do as I command. Take me to her."

In the courtyard, the clear-up had begun. Kangaroos and wallabies were collecting the corpses of the smaller creatures in their pouches, whilst a pair of huge lions were dragging the headless body of the giraffe back through the Palace gates.

From her vantage point Seward peered out into the stockade. The rhino was tied up and slumped in the furthest corner. With eyes half closed, she was lapping at what looked like an empty bowl.

Mrs Rhino wiped away a tear, "She was always fine. A perfect child A loyal respectable daughter. Until…. nectar."

Seward didn't comment. *If it was true that nectar was the reason, why had it not affected any other of her subjects?* She wanted to hear what the rhino had to say for herself. "Open up the stockade."

"I'm sorry, Your Majesty. Look around you," Plop swung his mighty head towards the carnage. "That animal has killed. It would be dangerous for us to open the gate."

"She's not dangerous," said Mother Rhino, "That's absurd."

"If she'd not been given…." Father Rhino contributed.

"I will not sanction it," Plop butted in.

"Well, I will." Seward's tone was firm and insistant.

Roly the Raccoon nervously intervened, "The beast is insane, Your Majesty…. It could cost more lives."

"Open them!" Seward shouted.

Plop waited, then reluctantly waved to the guards. The gates were opened and Plop cautiously stepped inside.

The rhino seemed unconcerned.

With his ears flapping with nervous energy, Plop circled slowly forward. Raising his trunk, he approached, step by step, then hesitated, "I fear it would be dangerous to get any nearer, Your Majesty."

"Nonsense! The beast is restrained. Closer. Closer, I command you."

Plop leant forward tentatively touching the ground with his trunk, and was about to take another step, when, in a flash the rhino was on her feet. She snapped the heavy ropes that had bound her, as though they were nothing more than cotton thread. With speed that belied her bulk, she charged. Plop did his best to fend off the rhino, but with Seward on his back, his mobility was compromised. Suddenly the rhino changed her position and with a vicious swipe, plunged her horn deep into the elephant's belly. With a shriek from Plop the guards rushed forward and after a bit of pushing and tussling managed to subdue the rhino.

Plop limped back through the gates.

"Oh dear, that was quite a fright," Seward giggled. "It gave me quite a start. I certainly wasn't expecting that. Great fun, what!"

Plops trunk went to his injured side, touching the gaping wound. He managed a chuckle, "Great fun, yes. I think so," then coughed. Moments later his legs gave way and he slumped to his knees.

"What's going on?" said Seward, annoyed at the sudden jolt. She stretched her left eye as far as she could. "I can't see, I can't see." Slithering up higher, she spotted blood dripping from Plop's side. "Oh, my goodness, what has happened?"

"I'm ok," said Plop, "Nothing to worry about." He let out a low rumble and with a groan slumped over to one side.

Roly the Raccoon dashed off, returning a few moments later with a blue pouch with a star on it, his medicine box. Frantically he attended to the fallen elephant.

One of the guards lifted Seward off Plop's shoulders,

"Your Majesty."

With his gaping wound now clearly visible, it was too much for the tiny snail, she swooned.

*

Back in the Royal Quarters Seward awoke. After a moment's recollection, she went over her thoughts. *Yes, it had happened. What about Plop? Was he ok? What had caused the rhino to commit such a murderous act?* But with every thread of understanding, the only thing in her mind's eye was the blood gushing from Plop's side. She took ten deep breaths and popped her head out of her shell. "Where is Plop?"

Roly put down the book he was reading, "You're awake, Your Majesty. Is there anything I can get you?"

"Where is Plop?"

Roly pulled back his lips, "He's in the courtyard, Your Majesty."

"Take me to him."

"Certainly!" Roly stood up, placed Seward onto a velvet cushion and carried her outside.

On spotting an elephant that she mistook for Plop; Seward felt a sense of relief.

The elephant turned; it wasn't Plop at all. He saluted, "Your Majesty."

"Where is Plop?" Seward asked anxiously.

The elephant looked confused.

"Where is he?"

The elephant pointed to the far side of the courtyard where a group of twelve elephants had gathered into a defensive circle. Soaring high above them circled ten hungry vultures, patiently waiting.

"Make way," called Roly. A gap opened.

Seward's heart leapt at seeing her old friend, but her joy was short-lived. There was something about how he was positioned. He was sprawled out, head over to one side, eyes distant, empty of thought and light. Whatever had once filled them was now gone.

"Plop, Plop," Seward called, "Plop, I command you to answer me... Now!" But, of course, there was no answer. The faithful elephant was dead.

Seward slithered up onto his huge grey head, and there she sat for hours, talking to the dead elephant until the moon showed itself, she then raised her eyes, "Kill the rhino."

At these words, the ten vultures dropped closer.

Tommy Turkey

Tommy Turkey woke, it was dark and still very early. Not wanting to wake his wife Agnes, he quietly slipped out of the nest and pecked at a scattering of seeds she'd laid out for breakfast. Just as he was about to leave Agnes stirred.

"What are you doing?" she asked.

"Nothing sweetie," Tommy gobbled across. "Just a little bit of business to take care of, I'll be back soon."

Still dozy, Agnes let out a snuffled gobble, turned over and went back to sleep.

"Gobble-gobble-gobble," Tommy Turkey was talking to himself on his way to see Pippa the Python. All was silent apart from the occasional crack of a twig underfoot

A neatly clipped hedge defined the boundary between Birdland and Reptile Land. Tommy glanced over his shoulder, then dipped through a hole in the hedge.

Reptile Land is a strange place, utterly different than you might expect. Now this is a strange thing, but for some reason, reptiles like straight lines and a lot of signage. Even today, if humans weren't around, reptiles would set up their areas grid-like. The idea being straightforward enough. As cold-blooded creatures, a reptile would warm up in the morning sunshine, and once their circulation got moving, off they go, following a sign directly to the nearest swamp to cool down. They're a lot more sophisticated than we give them credit for.

Tommy was no mug; there was a reason he'd set off so early. Number one, if caught in in anywhere other than Bird Land without the King's consent, it was a small cage and hard seed for a very long time. Number two, with the reptiles still sluggish or asleep, he was safe; why, a crocodile would gobble him down in one.

Flying up onto one of the signposts Tommy checked the map. His eyes searched the grid until he found Pippa's lair, the fourth tree along Python Avenue, Eastside. Five minutes later Tommy was at the base of an old rubber tree, Pippa's home. He flapped and flapped and managed to get airborne, landing on one of the lower branches, then climbed up the rest of the way. He looked up at the moon, it was just past forty-two o'clock, Pippa would not be up for at least another twelve hours, so finding a comfortable spot, he closed his eyes for a quick nap. Just as he was dropping off, he jerked back to life as a tiny gecko skipped over his feet, a large yellow lizard was on the gecko's heels. In the time it took to blink, the big lizard flicked out its long tongue and grabbed the little fella, then without saying grace or excuse me, chomped down his smaller friend in a couple of bites.

As Tommy looked on, the lizard's monstrous tongue again emerged, flicking over its eyes and lips. Then one eye rotated and fixed on our turkey friend. Tommy was aware that lizards are almost blind, and it was movement that got their attention, so if he stayed perfectly still and held his breath... The eye started at his turkey feet, travelled up his scaly legs, over his feathers and now was looking at him straight in the eye. Unfortunately for Tommy, as often happens when you need to be still, he felt a sneeze coming on. He tried to hold it in, but the tiniest gobble emerged. The other eye of the lizard spun a full 360 degrees. *Perfectly still, perfectly still,* Tommy said to himself. It was hard, because now it was an itchy beak. The reptiles tongue flicked out, once, twice, but whatever it tasted was unappealing and as quickly as it had arrived, it vanished in search of a second breakfast.

Tommy let go of his breath and gave his beak a good scratch.

It took a while for his eyes to adjust to the darkness of Pippa's lair. She was asleep in a hollow, her vast body coiled up, little piffles of snores coming from her dainty nose.

"Wakey, wakey," Tommy called out. Pippa didn't stir, "Wakey, wakey," he said louder, but still no response. Tommy nudged her scaly head with one of his clawed feet. Pippa opened one eye just ever so slightly, then closed it. He tried again, a proper kick this time, but it was no good; the sleepy snake would only wake when she was ready. Feeling himself at a loose end, Tommy went back outside and began breakfasting on the tree's delicious leaves. It wasn't long before something caught his eye.

Although some of my readers will no doubt find what the turkey did next amusing, I cannot condone or pardon it. I've only put it in to portray the true sense of the turkey's character and total disregard for his fellow creatures.

After eating so many leaves, Tommy's stomach had swollen enormously. It grumbled, then rumbled. The rumble quickly progressed; he had to go and go soon.

What had caught his eye was a tiny yellow tortoise. It was troubling no one, up early, going at its own pace across the jungle floor looking forward to the delicious fresh mushroom stalks that had cropped up in the night. Tommy smiled and repositioned himself on the branch directly above our little friend, and didn't that turkey let go of his innards, covering the little fella in a mess of turkey droppings. Disgusting I know, and if the little fella wasn't so covered in poop, it would have heard a wicked turkey gobbling in delight.

"Hisss, Hiiissssss!" came a sound.

Tommy hopped back inside to investigate.

"Oh, it's you," said Pippa, rubbing the sleep from her eyes with the end of her tail.

"Yes, it's me. You should have been awake a while ago. I told you I would be here early."

Pippa flicked out her tongue and shook a ripple through her body. She yawned, the foul smell of decomposing flesh on her breath. "What time is it?"

"Wakey-wakey time," grinned the turkey. "Come on, we've got business."

Pippa huffed, again flicking out her tongue. It was then Tommy noticed the shape lodged in her stomach; he winced.

"I'm ssstill tired. Can't you come back... laaater?"

"Nonsense, we've got plans to make. Wakey-wakey!" said Tommy plucking at his feathers. He counted out one hundred, then plucked out some more. "All you have to do is coat yourself in those. And we've got ourselves an unheavenly creature and a New King."

Pippa looked confused.

Tommy dragged a wing across his throat, and winked, "Now or never, eh!"

Still, Pippa wasn't on point, "Un...heaven...leee...cree-tures? What do you mean?"

Perhaps Pippa was not the trusty ally he once thought. With his patience wearing thin, Tommy replied, "You don't need to know; just be at the hole in the hedge at gobbledy-gobbledy-gook time." He pointed to the pile of discarded feathers, "Make sure you plaster those over your body, but not over your head. Is that clear?"

Pippa slid her tail around the turkey's shoulders and smiled, sending another blast of decaying odour towards Tommy. "What'sss... the time?"

Tommy shook his head in bewilderment, "Gobbledy-gobbledy-gook time…. Everything clear?"

Pippa nodded.

With a plan scant on detail, the turkey left the snake to her lie-in.

*

The position of the General of the Guard was passed from Plop to the next in line. Cindy was sixty-eight years old; stout, strong and extremely loyal. On the downside she was ponderously slow, short-sighted and prone to panic attacks.

It was early, the sun was shining on the Palace of Xum, a warm start for Seward's return to Bird Land to search for Tommy Turkey's mysterious unheavenly creatures. Cindy had selected for the journey five elephants, four camels, and a dozen meercat servants. As it was her first mission, she was nervous. After checking over every buckle and strap, then over again and again, she was ready.

Even keener to get going was Roly. The heat was getting to him, and the day was only going to get hotter.

Seward was escorted from the Palace and helped up onto Cindy's shoulders. The heavy gates opened, the drawbridge was lowered and the convoy slowly moved off. Although the sun was smiling, it scorched like a furnace. They should have reached Bird Land by early afternoon, but with water stops and the deadly slow pace Cindy set, it was well into the evening when they finally arrived. Exhausted, Seward put off her meeting with Tommy Turkey, she would rest first.

Roly too was worn out, but there was his duty, "Your Majesty, what time should I wake you? Remember we have the egg laying awards, the prettiest chick competition, then the feather inspection...." He was about to go on, but the little snail had retracted into her shell. Roly was relieved, he found a tall tree to shelter under and slumped down.

Just as he was dropping off, someone shouted, "Your lordship!"

Roly opened an eye to witness Tommy Turkey blustering his way through a huddle of hens.

But before the turkey arrived, a little pink sparrow landed alongside the racoon and saluted, saying, "Permission to speak, my lord?"

Roly wearily got to his feet.

The sparrow was about to go on, when Tommy Turkey flapped a wing and sent the little fellow sprawling. "I say, I've something to discuss with you," Then, as though forgetting himself, Tommy's tone changed to that of a funeral director, head to one side, wings clasped as though in prayer. He squeezed out a tear which struggled down his wrinkly cheek, "I'm so sorry to hear of the tragic news."

Roly's expression was that of a poker player.

Tommy squeezed out another tear and with an exaggerated sweep of his wing brushed it away, then let out a low mournful gobble, dropped his eyes and waited. A moment later he took a sly peek.

"What is it you want?" asked Roly sharply.

"Oh, I am sorry. I'm normally not this emotional. It's just that I was so fond of Plod." He took a deep breath. "Such a gentleman, an example to us all. I don't know if I'll ever get over his loss."

"You mean Plop?

Tommy seemed momentarily confused, his tongue wiped over his beak, and without a hint of embarrassment, "Yes, Plop, Plod… Plop, that's what I said."

Roly sneered and shook his head. *What was this bird after? Some plan, a proposition. Probably requesting selection onto the Bird Land Council. That would be about his limits. Maybe… yes, perhaps.*

As we know, Tommy Turkey's ambitions were greater than the council level, far, far greater indeed and his aim was to weave Roly into a web of treason. So hence he told the tale of the 'Unheavenly Creature.' A feathered snake with an otter's body, and centipede's legs, which slept through the day and feasted at night. If he could persuade Roly and then

Roly persuades the King. A hungry Python called Pippa would do the rest. It would be like taking worms from a duckling.

Roly was unconvinced; but wanted to know more. "Who else knows? When can we see it?" Roly smirked contemptuously, saying, "Perhaps it was just a snake?"

Feigning to be incensed by Roly's insinuation, Tommy spread his tail feathers and let out an angry gobble, "As sure as I'm standing here."

For an experienced operator like Roly, it was plain to see the turkey's face was filled with treason. Roly undoubtedly held rank, but power is an elusive commodity, often traded but impossible to measure. For now, he'd let him play his part. *Only when the mascarade is over do we reveal ourselves.*

*

Roly entered the Royal Quarters, stood to attention and saluted, then waited, "Your Majesty I have news."

Seward was enjoying a piece of corn. "I've never tried this before, have you? It's delicious," she looked up at Roly, "Try some." Seward nudged a piece over the platter, "There, try it."

As he looked down at the slime-covered kernel, Roly felt somewhat nauseous. Tapping his tummy, he grinned, "Erm, I'm not so very hungry, Your Majesty."

"Nonsense, try; it's delicious." Seward's tone was curt, brimming with authority. "We all should try new experiences, don't you agree?"

Bending closer, Roly sniffed at the kernel. He picked it up, and whilst his King looked on, swallowed it down in one. The slime wasn't as bad as he'd anticipated; if anything, it had a hint of strawberry. "Delicious," said Roly forcing a smile. He was about to speak when.

"Try another piece."

Roly did try another piece and when finished, made a point of licking his lips.

"I said you'd like it." Seward smiled, "Now, tell me, what's this news?"

Roly pushed out his chest and straightened his back, "I have now thoroughly investigated the matter and have spoken to the Turkey, Your Majesty. It would seem that there is indeed an unheavenly creature located on the borders between Bird land and Reptile Land."

Without realising how close she was to the edge of the platter, Seward craned towards a piece of corn, *only a fraction more*. As she took a bite, her body swayed, it went this way, then that, and before she knew it she'd lost her grip. Her shell hit the floor, rolled and ended up at Roly's feet.

Roly's initial reaction was to pick her up, but he froze. A delicious, devious, evil, monstrous thought slipped into his mind.

The King was frantically waving her tentacles, her tender body exposed.

Maybe this was his moment; one step would end it. *No, he couldn't... but then again, an opportunity like this...?* He furtively glanced over his shoulder, it was just him and the snail. With his heart beating frantically, he raised his foot.

When Roly came to, he was imprisoned in a bamboo cage. His head was throbbing and there was a strange strawberry taste in his mouth. All he could remember was talking to the King and a loud trumpet blast.

Cindy was haughtily marching back and forth, but seeing her captive conscious, she stopped, contemptuously announcing, "Roland Racoon, Adviser to the King, you have been relieved of your duties."

Roly didn't respond, he was foggy headed and blood was dripping from his nose. He rubbed his temple and winced. Like a thunderbolt, his senses returned. *Oh no! Oh no! It was just a thought; I would never...., just a thought, that's all.* "But I didn't do anything," he called out.

Cindy shook her head and fixed him with a glare, "That'll be for the courts to decide."

Roly felt outraged but knew to hold his tongue. *Best to say nothing.* He eased up onto his feet and took a tour of his gaol. It was about the size of a racoon lying down but was not quite high enough for him to stand. The floor was wooden and scattered with straw. He took a deep breath and sat back down. *I'll explain to the King, she'll understand. She's an example to us all, a champion of justice and mercy. The King knows I would never do anything to harm her.* In his mind, she was already accepting his apology.

*

"Yes, Your Majesty, I can show you," said Tommy Turkey pointing to an area on the map.

"Only a day's walk you say?" asked Seward.

"Yes, Your Majesty," replied Tommy.

Seward called for The Book of Unheavenly Creatures. Cindy fetched it and placed it in front of Seward and Tommy.

Page after page.

"Is it that one?" said Seward pointing at a picture, a snake with antlers.

"No, not quite, Your Majesty," Tommy hesitantly replied.

Cindy turned another page, then another. They stopped next at a fearsome-looking snake with spiders' legs and a rhinoceros horn.

Seward looked up.

"Not quite, but getting close," said Tommy.

"Feathers, you say?" Seward replied.

"Yes, an otter's body, feathers, a snake's head and tail, and legs of a centipede," Tommy reassured.

Seward thought for a moment, "And it sleeps during the day?"

"Yes, Your Majesty." Tommy was only half listening. With Roly's arrest, he was adjusting his plan. He blurted out, "We should go today before sunset. Your Majesty can then witness the abomination with her own eyes."

Seward raised an eyebrow, annoyed with the Turkey's impudence. She would say when they should or should not go. She went back to the book, "Is it that one? Or that one?" After going through the whole of The Book of Unheavenly Creatures, with a hesitant "No," from Tommy to every picture. She dismissed him and went for a rest. She'd hardly dropped off when she was woken by coughing and the tip of Cindy's trunk gently tapping her shell.

"What is it?"

"If we are to see the creature, we must head off. It will be dark soon, and if this creature is as savage as I think...."

"Fiddlesticks! I am the King; I'll go when I'm ready," said Seward crawling back into her shell. Moments later, tiny snores could be heard.

Cindy bowed deeply and left the room.

The Beast

Tommy was skipping along enjoying himself, dodging between the trees and overhanging vines. "This way, Your Majesty,".

In contrast, Cindy was puffing and blowing. She was not liking the pace at all. To her, the route seemed far too elaborate; back and forth, back and forth, and if memory served her right, they'd passed the fallen baobab tree at least three times. "How much further?"

Tommy glanced back, "Not long now." He suddenly jolted to a halt, raised a wing and cautiously sniffed the air.

Cindy pulled up alongside him.

"Can you get that?" Tommy sniffed, his face showing concern.

Cindy raised her trunk high, wafting it back and forth, but couldn't smell anything apart from the Turkey and lush vegetation.

Tommy sniffed again and followed it up with a knowing nod, then cautiously moved forward.

"What's happening?" asked Seward.

"I think we are near the creature's lair, Your Majesty," said Cindy, placing her huge feet onto the tracks left by the turkey. Cindy's heart was pounding; she was never keen on snakes at the best of times, never mind one with an otter's body, feathers and a hundred legs.

As if on cue, a parrot squawked; Cindy squealed, and whether it was in her control or not, she ran, knocking Tommy Turkey flying, straight through the boundary hedge and into Reptile Land.

At the sound of her screams, Pippa the Python peeked out from her feathery hideout, seeing the crazed elephant heading her way, she slid away as fast as her slippery body could carry her. The last thing she wanted was to be crushed underfoot.

Branches flew as Cindy ran in circles, letting out trumpet calls that could be heard from miles away. Around and around, she went, it was all Seward could do to hold on. In fact, the King thought they were in the midst of a hurricane or tornado.

Tommy let out a screeching gobble, the signal for Pippa to appear. But with Cindy running amok, there was no way that Pippa was going to show herself. Tommy Turkey could take a flying jump; she'd wait and watch.

Cindy's rampage went on until every piece of vegetation surrounding her was either broken, shredded or flattened. She looked nervously around, then took a deep breath, then another and slowly she felt calmer. Her trunk reached up to check on Seward, who although upside down, was still there. Relieved, Cindy smiled an embarrassed smile.

Not everyone knows this, but when elephants panic they often get hiccups, and that's precisely what happened here. Cindy's breath skipped, her belly wobbled, and her head shook.

"What on earth is going on now?" Seward called out.

"Nothing, Your Majesty. A little stumble, nothing to worry about," said Cindy her face contorted as she tried holding her breath. But as hiccup after hiccup emerged, each one sent a shudder through her body, throwing Seward high up into the air. Cindy even tried plugging her trunk into her mouth, but it was no good, "Hiccup, hiccup...." It was like a rodeo ride for poor little Seward as she was bumped and jostled like never before.

Tommy quickly recognised the elephant's predicament and began frantically running around calling, "A good slap on the back, a good slap on the back," hoping that Cindy would shake Seward loose, and if it wasn't an elephant's foot that crushed the

King, who would know if it was a turkey's? "The Beast! The Beast!" he shouted, pointing at a moss-covered branch "The Beast!"

Cindy let out an even bigger trumpet call, squealed, and around and around again they went. Catching hold of the branch, she bashed it hard against a tree and then swung it with all her might high into the sky. Seward, Tommy, Pippa, and Cindy all watched as the branch spun like the blades of a helicopter over the hedge of Reptile Land and into Bird Land.

"Oh dear, I think I might have killed it. I think I might have killed it!" Cindy cried out, as she gulped for breath.

"Calm down, I command you. Calm down!" Seward shouted.

Tommy was still thrashing around like a maniac, "The Beast! The Beast!"

"Stop it! Stop it! said Seward, "That wasn't a creature; it was a branch. I know a branch when I see one. I've crawled over them many a time."

From her hideout, Pippa was grinning, she would have laughed aloud if she could, but as snakes can't laugh, she let out a jolly hisss.

"I'm sure it was alive, Your Majesty. It tried to bite

me," said Cindy, looking to Tommy for confirmation.

Tommy was scratching around, kicking up leaves and twigs. He had one eye on the jungle floor whilst the other was searching for Pippa. "I'm not sure, Your Majesty. It didn't look exactly like the unheavenly creature, but it certainly terrified, he glanced at Cindy and raised an eyebrow, The General of the Guard."

*

Back in Bird Land, it took Tommy only a short time to find the offending article. "Just as you said, Your Majesty, a branch. An old, harmless branch," he gobbled with glee.

After inspecting the phoney beast, Seward ordered them back to camp.

As they returned Tommy began singing a quickly made-up song, "Just a branch, bum bum. Just a branch, bum bum. Just an old branch, for a scaredy pants."

Cindy's tail was flicking in anger, a quick swipe with her trunk would finish him off, but she didn't say a word.

*

Tommy was still singing his song when they arrived

back. Birds of all types had gathered, all expecting to see the elusive unheavenly creature. Madame Ostrich welcomed the King with a freshly picked onion. But Seward was far too furious to think about food and angrily waved the huge bird away.

As they passed Roly in his gaol, the raccoon stood, puffed out his chest and saluted, "Your Majesty."

Tommy Turkey was never known as tight-beaked, and by the time darkness had fallen, every bird in Bird Land was laughing at the thought of The General of the Guard being scared of an old mossy branch.

A Decree of Purity

Same as today, in the animal Kingdom, loose tongues and idle chatter were a daily part of courtly life. Nifty ferrets, with their slim wriggly bodies, wagging tongues and beady eyes, were the worst, they loved nothing better than to gossip. They seemed to know everything, and if they didn't, they were happy to embroider a tale. The ferrets were the source of such stories as the hippos were organizing a secret wallow party, frogs were savaging newts, and devious owls were plotting against zebras, just general gossip, truth or lies, who would know? But even the ferrets did not have the answer to the number one subject of the day. *Why was the King so concerned about Unheavenly Creatures?*

Seward wanted proof one way or the other, of whether Unheavenly Creatures ever truly existed, and if so, why were they no longer around? Each night after supper, she'd disguise herself as a common snail and slither off to the library, crawling over book after book in the hope of finding something. It didn't take her long to unearth the Document of Species, which detailed all the possible liaisons to be outlawed but it lacked any evidence as to why. In Abraham the

Donkey's diary, there was mention of a cricket with the ears of a hare and of a cat with shrimp's whiskers but it was written as though part of a story. Night after night she returned going through document after document, until finally she found what she was looking for. At the back of a cupboard, she came across a bundle of dusty scrolls, so old they were almost falling apart. One in particular caught her eye, it wa titled The Decree of Purity.

The Decree of Purity

In this year of Higgledy-Piggledy, in the Kingdom of Xum

To maintain Purity of Spirit and Blood

We the nobles agree to designated borders.

It was signed by the appointed leaders.

Seward was furious, such a major pronouncement, in so few lines, with no explanation, there had to be more. She slithered over a document from the bees, a final   demand for payment for an unpaid bill for two hundred gallons of nectar. Then she found it.

The proclamation of King Aloysius.

In this year of Topsy-Turvy

Polypious God of all Gods has delivered his judgement

The Kingdom of Xum is awash with corruption and degeneration

Species beyond Species.

Caste beyond Caste

Linage beyond Linage

Denomination beyond Denomination

Province beyond Province

Hierarchy beyond….

As Seward read, the scroll began to crumble, falling to the floor as snowy ash. Seward moved on to an agreement, a contract between Polypious, God of all Gods, and King Aloysuis, but no sooner had Seward begun to read, then that too turned into ash. The same with the next scroll and the one after that.

Unbeknownst to Seward, Polypious God of all Gods had been watching. He knew exactly what was about to be revealed and was ashamed of the price he paid for worship and devotion.

Roly's Trial

"Bring forth the witness," said the owl glancing over his half-rimmed spectacles.

"Calling Blinky the Meerkat," said the usher, a drab-looking pigeon with only one eye, who was acting for both the defence and the prosecution.

Blinky made his way through a gaggle of geese and scrambled up onto the witness perch.

"Take this egg," said the pigeon holding forth a blue speckled one. "Do you solemnly flap to peck the truth, the whole truth and nothing but the truth?"

Confused, Blinky looked to the judge.

"Just wave your arms and nod," said the wise owl reassuringly.

"But your worship," the pigeon cooed, irate at the deviation from official court procedure.

"Get on with it," said the owl, dismissing him.

Roly was watching intently from his gaol at the back of the court. He was hoping for a procedural error that would warrant an appeal if his case did not go as he wished, and had already marked that one down.

Seward was on her throne, high up on Cindy's shoulders. They had prime position, just to the right of the judge and away from the hoi polloi. Both were due to give evidence later. The jury, perched along a long winding branch were made up of three parrots, four white doves, an ostrich, two peacocks, six blue tits, twenty-three colourful hens, and a loud-mouthed cockerel. Oh yes, I forgot, there was one other member on the jury, a turkey called Tommy.

"Can you please convey to the court exactly what you witnessed on the day of the alleged crime?" said the pigeon with a theatrical wave of its wing.

A nervous Blinky began, his eyelids going from a trot to a gallop. "Well, I was on my way to…"

"Objection!"

The jury's eyes shot to the back of the room.

"Objection," Roly repeated.

"Objection? Objection?" the judge peered down from his perch, "Twit-twit-twoo, are you. What do you object toooo?"

"My Lord, I would like to address the court, if I may,"

Roly responded.

"I'm addressing you, twit-twoo, and suggest you shut up, until spoken to," said the judge, fixing Roly with a scowl.

Roly looked suitably chastised.

"Go on," said the judge to Blinky.

Surprisingly, in contrast to his lively eyelids, Blinky's tone was slow and measured, "I was on my way to deliver a message.... to the King... and about to enter.... the royal quarters... but hearing voices.... I waited...." Blinky looked to Roly at the back of the court, stared for a moment, then looked back to the judge. "There was a low rumble noise.... from behind me.... a moment later," Blinky looked at Cindy, stared, then back at the judge.

"Go on, go on," said the owl, somewhat perturbed at Blinky's lack of pace.

"Fearing a telling off from the General of the Guard for loitering... I immediately pulled back the curtain and entered the royal quarters. I heard a noise... A funny noise... Tap, tap... clickity-clack."

"Tap, clickity clack," said the one-eyed pigeon, turning to the jury.

"No," answered Blinky. He peered up at Seward, stared, then back to the judge, "Tap, tap… clickity-clack."

"Ahh, tap, tap, clickity clack," repeated the one-eyed pigeon smiling, "I stand corrected."

Tommy Turkey looked along the jury branch, and although nowhere near the Royal Quarters at the time, nodded vigorously, confirming Blinky's statement.

"An….d! What happened next?" asked the pigeon.

"I tiptoed as quietly as I could." Blinky looked at his feet, took a breath or two, as though building up courage. His paw went out, pointing directly at Roly, "He was over the King, and was going to kill her!"

The court erupted with clucks, squarks, hoots and trills.

The Judge slammed his conker gavel on his perch, "Order! Order I say!"

Tommy glared at Roly, and gobbled out, "Murderer." Then got to his feet and pointed directly at the racoon, "Murderer!" he repeated.

The court erupted with wings flapping and feathers flying. It was all the judge could do to keep control.

Next on the witness perch were Cindy and Seward together. Obviously, they didn't perch; well, who's ever seen an elephant on a perch? Cindy spoke honestly saying, she hadn't actually seen anything prior to Blinky's scream, but on entering the Royal Quarters, she could see Roly the Racoon hovering over the King.

"Did you know the accused's intentions?" asked the one-eyed pigeon.

Cindy looked to the judge, "In all honesty my Lord, I could not say."

Seward's evidence was very scant. Yes, she has inadvertently slipped, but she was unaware of the Advisor to the Kings actions. For some reason, she added, "Although, I feel he may have wanted to hurt me."

The judge thanked the King, saying he was very grateful to her for having delivered her evidence so clearly and concisely. He then asked for a round of applause, no-one was clapping harder than Roly.

Seward waved a tentacled eye, "Thank you. The pursuit of truth and justice is a noble endeavour that we must all aspire to."

"Next witness," called the one-eyed pigeon.

Roly was released from his gaol and escorted by a pair of penguins to the front. With a bit of an effort and a lot of wobbling, he climbed up onto the witness perch and was sworn in. His evidence was very much biased; even I could tell that. It went something like this; he had no intention of harming Seward or anyone. Why, he would sacrifice his own life for his King, yawdie-yardee-yah… all very predictable. He said due to the excessive slipperiness of the corn cob, and that unfortunately the King had lost her balance and slipped. "It could have happened to anyone, Your Majesty," Roly stated and bowed in Seward's direction, his paw covering his heart. The only reason his foot was out, was to break the King's fall, and if he hadn't been there, it was very likely Her Majesty may have been injured or even worse. He finished by saying, "That meerkat only witnessed the tail end of events, so to speak. No pun intended."

"Liar," shouted Tommy Turkey.

The cockerel crowed out a cockle doodle-doo. The rest of the jury joined in, particularly the hens, who clucked and clucked such vicious phrases that I couldn't possibly repeat here.

Tommy smiled, crossed his wings and sat back, as the ruckus developed.

"Quiet, quiet! Quiet in my court!!!" said the owl,

slamming the conker down, "Quiet!"

But the mayhem continued until Cindy let fly a screeching trumpet blast.

As they settled, the judge scanned the jury branch, glaring at each bird, until the squabbling completely subsided. "The witness may be returned."

Before being led back to his gaol, Roly bowed before the jury, the judge, and particularly to Seward.

The owl judge closed his huge eyes for what seemed like an eternity; clearly, he was cogitating. Seward had moved as far as she dared along Cindy's head, transfixed as she awaited the decision.

After what seemed like an eternity, the judge opened his eyes and blinked three times, which was traditional when making an important legal statement. The court hushed. He cleared his throat, then spoke, "I have carefully listened to the evidence, and although there are suspicions. I have not heard any solid evidence of the intention of the accused to murder or harm our King. The witnesses have been very clear. Even the King herself could not categorically say that the accused was about to assault her. I only have Blinky the Meerkat's view that a crime 'may' have been about to be committed."

You will no doubt be asking, dear reader, what is the

point of the jurors? Well, in Bird Land, jurors weren't selected to make any legal decisions. No, they were chosen simply to add colour and song to a very dull day's proceeding.

Sensing he was about to be set free, Roly grinned. He felt a weight lifted from his shoulders and was beaming from ear to ear.

"Trial by standing," called Tommy, "Let him stand trial by standing."

This was followed by a cockle-doodle-doo from the loudmouth cockerel. The hens joined in, clucking, "Trial by standing."

Again, this trial, test, call it what you may, was a peculiarity to Bird Land. If enough birds demanded, and the judge agreed, an accused could be asked to stand on one leg for one whole night. The thought was that only the innocent could stand on one leg for such an extended length of time.

Roly was confused; it was all new to him. Grabbing the bars of his cage he stared wide eyed at the judge.

The judge glared down at Tommy the Turkey, "Nonsense, the accused is not a bird and could not be expected to stand on one leg throughout the night.... Motion denied." He clapped the conker down, "The defendant is free to go."

"What about two legs?" Tommy called out.

"My decision is final." The owl judge bowed to Seward, "Your Majesty," and with a flap of his wings he took to the air and disappeared silently into the jungle.

Case concluded.

The court was in consternation; none could believe what had happened. There were claims of a set-up, some sort of deal.

Seward tapped Cindy's shoulder, the sign for her to be taken to her quarters.

Roly emerged from his gaol with a swagger, prancing back and forth in front of the enraged jury. Only cutting short his celebration as one of the guards let out a trumpet blast. "The court is now closed."

That evening there was a decision to be made, a difficult one at the best of times, but considering what Roly had been accused of, one of national security. The question was whether Roly the Racoon should reassume his position as Advisor to the King. A job, it must be said, he'd worked diligently at for previous Kings and Queens for years. Cindy was dead against it; the risk was just too much; she didn't trust the racoon. Seward called for Blinky the meerkat, asking him to go over every detail of what he had witnessed.

She then called in every staff member of the Palace; had anyone heard any whispers of treachery or betrayal? After questioning all and sundry, Seward was none the wiser.

The following day Roly was summoned. Cindy frisked him down and, once satisfied, waved him forward.

With a click of his heels, he marched confidently toward the King and performed a deep bow, "At your service, Your Majesty."

Seward asked for all apart from Roly to leave the Royal Tent; she wanted to question him alone.

Cindy was reluctant to leave the two alone and protested, but Seward insisted. Cindy didn't go far however; staying just out of sight, with her ear pressed against the walls of the canopy. She was soon joined by Blinky who poked his head under the hem to sneak a peek.

Seward's eyes were wandering back and forth, examining the racoon, how did he look? How did he hold himself? Did he look guilty? Her ears too were alert, listening for a shortness of breath, a change of heartbeat, or maybe a shuffle of his feet, but as yet there was nothing.

To Roly's consternation, the watching and listening

went on for some time. He knew he must remain cool. He was reporting for duty, ready to serve his King. "Permission to speak, Your Majesty?"

Seward's scolding stare held the racoon in check, she'd let him stew a while longer.

What's going on? asked Cindy frustratedly.

Blinky ducked back, "Nothing much."

Roly stood in the awkward silence. *What was the King thinking? Was that glance an insight, a clue as to her thoughts?*

Seward remained icy cool, letting the time tick on, until she finally spoke, "A wrong forgiven is knowledge, but to forget is foolish."

The statement confused Roly, he waited a moment before hesitantly answering, "I fully agree, Your Majesty."

Blinky shuffled back under the curtain, "They're speaking."

Cindy slid her trunk under, and could taste the racoon's fear floating in the air, she smiled.

Despite what Cindy could detect with her extraordinary sense of smell, it wasn't apparent to

Seward. Although his mind was racing in ragged corners, Roly looked the picture of justified innocence.

"Kneel before your King," Seward commanded.

Roly knelt onto one knee, and lowered his eyes.

"I could have you banished, tortured, or even executed." Seward stretched forward and raised her head, "Why, even now if I…. decide," Her tone was flippant yet threatening. "Your death…. A mere…" Seward absently rubbed at a mark on her shell.

With his sail wind fading by the second, Roly glanced up.

"Do not look at me until instructed."

He dropped his head, his jaunty confidence only propped up by his whiskers.

"What's going on now?" Cindy whispered.

"The King is going to execute him," Blinky replied.

Cindy's trunk delved deeper inside and she took another sniff. Roly's fear was alive and swimming, it spotted Cindy's snake-like trunk and intrigued, made a beeline. Once inside, it spread through her body, touched her heart and gripped her soul, and then emerged as a terrified trumpet blast.

As though on cue, a burly guard smashed though the Royal Quarters, and not waiting for an explanation, pinned Roly to the ground with his arms twisted up behind his back.

Roly screamed, "Let me go, I haven't done anything, I haven't…."

"Stop! Stop," shouted Seward. "What are you doing?"

The guard looked to Cindy.

"Release him, I command you, release him," said Seward, her anger as palpable as Roly's fear.

The guard looked again to Cindy.

Cindy nodded, "Do as your King instructed."

Roly was lifted to his feet, and patted down by way of an apology.

Seward shouted as loud as her tiny voice could convey and stamped her foot, "All of you get out! Get out now!"

Alone she pondered, she was at her wit's end; what was she to do? Her chief advisor may have tried to kill her. The General of the Guard seemed to have a mania for panicking at the slightest thing, and then there was the turkey which she was sure was up to some sort of mischief. She curled into her shell, in the hope sleep would rescue her from her woes.

The Cloak of Destiny

"Luckily for you, I was there," said Tommy, easing up alongside Roly. "Without..." he was about to go on but was halted in his tracks.

"What do you mean?" Roly, his face twisted with disdain, "It was you who called me a murderer."

Tommy laughed light-heartedly, "It was a ploy. You can't seriously believe I meant it." He chuckled, "A ploy!"

Roly considered himself a good judge of character and didn't trust Tommy, but his mind was spinning.

Tommy went on, "The problem is, you don't know the lay of the land around here. Everyone knows that the cockerel and the judge don't get on." Tommy shrugged, "No one knows why exactly but if you ask me, it started when that cockerel more than ruffled Mrs Owls' feather." Tommy nudged Roly's ribs, his grin turned to a lecherous cackle, "If you get what I mean?"

Being a confirmed bachelor with no thoughts of change, Roly found talk of the birds and the bees quite disgusting, it was all a bit mucky for his liking. He frowned, his expression sour.

"You don't get it, do you?" Tommy changed his tone, "If I could get the hens and cockerel to go one way, I knew as sure as a chick's gonna cheep, that owl judge would do the opposite." He was remonstrating as though he was talking to a child. "Why do you think the judge flew off without any explanation…. Because, once those hens…. wagging tongues and all that!" Tommy glanced at Roly, whose colour was changing by the second, "What's up, fella? You one of those sensitive types?"

To stop from fainting, Roly put his head between his knees; he was trying to collect his thoughts. *Was he to believe this treacherous turkey? Absolutely not, but maybe, there was some strange logic...*

Tommy waited a moment then gave Roly a gentle kick, "Listen, we both weren't hatched yesterday. I'm the last to point a feather, but if you did…"

Roly looked indignant. "I think you'll find I was found not guilty."

Tommy shrugged, "I'm just saying," he fixed an eye on Roly for a moment as though considering, "Well, all I'm saying is I could fully understand." Glancing around, Tommy took a deep breath; he was about to

take the biggest gamble of his life. "What if I said....
the snail was due an unfortunate accident? How
would you feel about becoming King with me as your
advisor?"

Of course, Tommy had no intention of playing second
fiddle, but he fully understood the attraction of a
dangled carrot, particularly to a power-hungry racoon.
He waited a moment allowing his words to settle.
Then decided, in for a penny... "I have connections in
Reptile Land who I can rely on..." he slowly drew a
wing across his throat and winked at Roly, "All hail
Good King Roly."

What was Roly to do? *Could this turkey be
suggesting what he thought he was suggesting? It was
madness, yet his days as the King's advisor certainly
seemed numbered, especially if that number was zero.
An alliance may be the way forward.* With options
running out, Roly replied, "Let's walk."

Deeper into the jungle they went to weave a blanket
of deceit.

*

Seward blinked and opened her eyes. For a moment
she thought she was back at the Palace, with her
home comforts, beautiful gardens, flowers, and
strawberries, but as the cock crowed, her heart sank,

remembering she was still in Bird Land.

"Your Majesty," It was Cindy, she looked downcast and troubled.

"You may speak."

"I know I may have caused you dismay over the short while I have served. I want to apologise and... make a formal request to be relieved of my duties," Cindy was standing, trunk raised in a salute, "I remain your humble servant." Cindy's distress was plain to see, her eyes and the tip of her trunk both red from crying.

Seward knew this was unprecedented, The General of the Guard doesn't resign, they are only ever replaced on death. Seward's heart went to her, "Please relax. Let's not be rash. You are my servant. One whom I can trust and whose loyalty knows no bounds."

Cindy's shoulders heaved as she attempted to stifle a sob.

"There, there. No need for tears," Seward smiled warmly and waited as Cindy composed herself, "Nevertheless, I think we can both acknowledge... And who knows why, but you do tend to... shall we say... poop yourself at the slightest shock."

Cindy chuckled at the King's directness.

Seward spoke, "Something came to me in my dreams last night." Before going on, she paused as a distant memory scrambled through her thoughts…. then shook herself back to reality. "Tonight, you must undertake a challenge of what is real and what is unreal, a challenge of perception and discernment. It will reveal whether you can distinguish between the tangible and the illusory."

Cindy didn't quite understand the long words, but saluted.

"I will give you clearer instructions later, but for now you are dismissed."

Once Cindy left, Seward sent for Blinky, instructing him to go to the weaver birds. They were to weave a cloak large enough for an elephant. It was to be made from feathers so fine that the slightest breeze would set them free, and woven within it dried seeds of violets, and eggshells.

As evening approached, Blinky returned to the Royal Quarters leading a band of servants and the cloak was laid out. Seward could not fail to be impressed. It was more beautiful than she could ever have imagined, a cacophony of reds, greens and yellows, with seedpods of gold and bronze, all embroidered with blue shells.

Blinky smiled proudly, "It was me who advised on

the colours, Your Majesty."

"You chose well," Seward's eyes lingered over the garment, inspecting every feather, every seedpod, and shell. Once sated, her mind returned to the task at hand. She turned to Blinky, "Bring me the General of the Guard." The meercat scampered off.

At the sight of the shimmering cloak, Cindy trumpeted an ear-splitting alarm.

Seward winced, and once her ears stopped ringing, "There is nothing to worry about. It's merely a cloak. Come, come," she said, imploring Cindy, "Come forward, inspect it."

A feather floated into the air. Cindy stepped back, her ears wide and alert as she nervously eyed the dangerous feather.

Seward tried again, "Come, come."

Hesitantly Cindy stepped forward, her trunk swinging like the pendulum of a clock. She cautiously touched and sniffed the cloak. Another feather flew; Cindy pulled away sharply, watching and waiting, mesmerised as the feather floated then drifted to the ground.

"You see, there is nothing to be frightened of."

Cindy took another sniff and once satisfied that the cloak wouldn't attack, she smiled. "It's just feathers and seed pods."

"And eggshells," Seward added reassuringly.

After an age of cajoling, Seward convinced Cindy to wear the wonderous garment. If you have ever seen an Indian elephant in full ceremonial cape and regalia, you will have an idea. Cindy looked magnificent, absolutely breathtaking, if somewhat uncomfortable.

"If you would care to count the egg shells, you will find one hundred," said Seward.

Cindy did indeed count, her trunk sniffing and touching each shell softly and deliberately.

Seward waited, "Cindy, I do not doubt your loyalty, but loyalty is not enough for your position. You need to be able to care for and defend your King, and currently, I cannot say in all confidence you are able." She looked at the cloak, "This is your cloak of destiny. It is a chance to prove that you are truly, The General of the Guard."

Cindy's eyes widened, and her ears flapped forward.

"This night you must travel to the Royal Palace of Xum wearing this cloak. When you arrive there, strike the Bell of Knowledge, not once, not twice, but three times, then return to me by morning." Seward's tone changed, "I warn you there will be many trials to overcome. You will experience fear, but will learn never to be a slave to it again."

Cindy's Odyssey

Madame Ostrich had arranged an evening of entertainment, a night of song and dance for the King's final night in Bird Land. Seward was seated front row central, surrounded by the dignitaries of Bird Land.

The compere climbed up onto the stage, deliberately tripping on the steps, which always got him a laugh. He bowed to the audience and introduced himself as Billy Blackfoot, then began, "On my way here tonight…. You should see my wife… My mother-in-law…" that sort of thing, but then moved on to the harder stuff with a string of lewd jokes, and soon had his audience in stitches. But not everyone was enjoying the humour, Seward found him uncouth and vulgar, and let it be known by retracting into her shell, something which didn't go unnoticed. With a vigorous flap of her wings, Madame Ostrich quickly brought the curtain down on Billy Blackfoot's smut.

Whilst they waited for the next act, Madame Ostrich climbed up on to stage and performed an impromptu performance of her soft shoe shuffle, a Bird Land favourite. The audience quickly got into the swing, and were clapping along, but Seward still wasn't impressed. As far as she was concerned the ostrich's rhythm and timing were out and her feathers looked a mess. Seward yawned, and when no one noticed, she coughed, then began laughing as loud as she could. Eyes switched from the performance and onto the King. Madame Ostrich thought that the Seward was cheering, so she slung in a few extra moves, a step-heel and a couple of leap shuffles. But as howls of laughter began ringing in her ears, the penny dropped. Poor Madame Ostrich's tap became a thud, a slide, a skid, and her shuffle, a clumsy plod. The crestfallen bird cut short her performance, quickly bowed to the King, and promptly disappeared into the wings.

The next act was a choir of blackbirds. After introducing themselves as The Lucky Ten, they regally bowed to Seward. They began with delicate sweet harmonies, then the lead came in with a voice so pure, true and mellow.

Seward's head swayed as her thoughts drifted. Had she had heard the song before?

The Lucky Ten were joined by canaries, who added melodic tones to the already beautiful song. From overhead came the sound of thrushes and warblers, providing pitch and tempo. The sound was magical, heavenly. After a performance of about an hour they bowed to rapturous applause.

Billy Blackfoot returned to the stage grinning like a naughty schoolboy, he'd obviously been warned. This time he kept his jokes clean and told a lovely story about an albatross who made friends with a hummingbird. He then introduced a dance group of cranes and pink flamingos. Under the glow of the moon their movement traced out a tragic tale of love and loss. Their silent bodies gracefully expressing hope, sorrow and heartache. The audience was spellbound. Seward shed a tear as they finished and rose to give them a standing ovation.

Next on stage were The Four Mynah Birds, who performed their big hits; *The Bird and Other Bird, Peck If You Want to Go Faster,* and *Why Walk When You Can Fly.* Which all went down well. After leaving the stage, they came back for an encore, singing their most recent release, *Flap Me If You Can.*

Seward politely tapped her foot, but wasn't a great fan.

*

The night was still with just the tiniest wisp of a breeze when Cindy pulled The Cloak of Destiny around her and slipped away. She had made her mind up not to rush, every step, every breath was considered, a foot raised, a breath taken, then foot down and breath released. One after another, one after another, she pressed forward. She was well out of camp when behind her came the sound of a crack. She slowly turned her head, then let out a sigh of relief, it was only a twig. *Just a twig, just a twig, onwards!*

The moon smiled down as she let out a low rumble and picked up her pace. Further into the jungle she travelled, not one of the eggshells had yet been broken, or a feather lost. She was feeling confident and began humming that old traditional elephant tune, 'Two Tusks Are Better Than One.' It was then that something flashed at the side of her eye and touched her eyelid, soft and fleeting, then again it happened. Her heart jumped, and although her brain told her to relax, her feet had made up their minds and were up to a gallop, as on she raced to escape the fiery phantom of green and yellow, spitting seed of fire, and laughing with cackles of glee.

We, of course, know it wasn't a phantom, ghost or a monster. It was little more than The Cloak of Destiny, shedding feathers and seedpods. But fear is clever; even when we're sure there's nothing to be frightened of, it still manages to scare us.

By the time Cindy had slowed and calmed herself, the cloak was in shreds. To say the feathers were patchy would be an understatement. All that was left of the shells were five on her right-hand side, none on her rear, and two on her left. Feeling exhausted she sat down on the jungle floor, and dabbed at her tears. A single feather fluttered in front of her, she picked it up and tickled her eyelids, it felt nice. A loud quack made her look up. Across from her was a bright red duck staring at her.

"What are you doing?" the ducked quacked.

A little taken aback, Cindy waited before answering, "King's business," her tone gruff and officious.

"What business is that then?"

Cindy rubbed her chin with her trunk, "Aren't you supposed to be at the concert?"

The duck answered flippantly, "Nah, I don't like music." He made a kissing sound with his bill. "Common misconception."

"What?"

"That all birds like music. Especially their sort," the duck nodded in direction of the camp. "It drives me quackers. All that, tweet, tweet, tweet, never a quack-quack-quack." He blew out a whistle, "Let me introduce myself, Slapper the name, and dreaming is my game." He waddled closer, and began checking Cindy over, "Jeepers, you're a big one, and what the heck are you wearing?" he asked, nibbling at the feathers. Slapper looking up at Cindy, scratched his head, and pointed at her ears, "You'll never get off the ground with those." Pleased with his joke, he let out a chorus of throaty quacks.

Slapper was very talkative and very open, telling Cindy all about himself, his life as a duckling, the pond he lived in, how he'd been married eight times. He didn't know how many children he'd had but guessed five hundred, shrugging, "Far too many to get a fix on." But he'd left that all behind him now and had chosen the life of a hermit. His aim in life now was to find his spiritual guide. "It could be you," he winked. "No, I've had enough of their chitter-chatter," his head swung toward Bird Land.

Cindy explained that she was General of the Guard to the King, reaffirming she was on important King's business.

Slapper didn't seem impressed, but was interested in The Cloak of Destiny. He waddled over and began inspecting it.

There's a well-known saying in Bird Land, 'Curiosity Tangled the Duck,' and that's exactly what happened here. The more Slapper inspected, the more he got tangled. Feathers flew, seedpods cracked, he'd quack-quack-quack, flap for all he was worth and get even more snarled.

"Can you stop doing that?" said Cindy, as she tugged the cloak from beneath him.

"Hey, hold on a minute," cried Slapper. "No need to get physical; I was only straightening a few loose feathers."

"Stop, stop. Stop it," Cindy cried.

"Quack-quack-quack," Slapper struggled on and on until the beautiful cloak was a tangled mass of feathers and shattered eggshells. "Quaaack! Quaaack!"

Cindy's heart sank, "What have you done?"

"What's that crazy outfit all about anyway?" said Slapper, spitting out a feather.

"The Cloak of Destiny! The King gave it to me."

"The cloak of what? It just looks so…" Slapper was searching for a word. He waited and waited for the right word…. "Quaaack!"

"You don't understand," said Cindy.

"And what's all this business here?" said Slapper pecking at the few remaining shells.

Cindy's thoughts were in disarray. *Should she go on? Maybe it made more sense to turn back and explain to the King what had happened.* She felt like crying and tried, but only managed a feathery snort, followed by a very loud sneeze.

Slapper stopped grooming his feathers, and waddled closer, "Hey now, it's not the end of the world. I've seen the end of the world once before," he paused, "Yeah, way back, and it was nothing like this." Slapper began, "This stuff gets everywhere." He pecked at a shell and asked, "King? Which King are we on now? Good King Wenceslas? Henry Longbone? Philias the Mad?"

*

Seward looked up at the stars. The concert was coming to a close; she was tired and wanted her bed, but there was still one act to go.

Billy Blackfoot strolled back onto the stage, "My friends, I hope you've enjoyed yourselves tonight. I think you will all agree with me, that we have witnessed some of the best that music and dance have to offer." He waited for the applause to die down, "Our final act is a big star, a name you will be familiar with, who especially asked to perform for our gracious King tonight." Billy bowed, raised a wing and waved to the side of the stage, "Please welcome… Norris…. The King of Swing Nightingale!"

To cheers, raucous tweets and whistles, a rather dull-looking grey and brown bird flew to the centre of the stage. Norris bowed, to the left, to the right, then took a deep bow just for Seward, who regally waved one of her tentacles. When a hush descended Norris waltzed slowly across the stage, it was in this silence that he captivated his audience. From one side to the other, he danced, then back to the centre. Norris began with gentle soprano undertones that weaved their way through the audience and out into the jungle. He introduced melodious warbles to his repertoire. His song was unhurried, haunting and unworldly.

Seward was entranced, and it was at that very moment she realised she was in love. Whether with Norris or his song, she did not know, but there was a strange feeling rushing through her breast, tingling and caressing every sinew. For sure, it was love.

*

Slapper waddled off; then looked back. "What are you waiting for?"

Was Slapper telling her to follow? Or was it some cryptic message? Maybe Slapper wasn't there at all. Maybe Cindy herself wasn't there either?

"Get off your backside," the duck quacked forcefully.

The spell was broken. Cindy got to her feet and followed Slapper to a narrow pathway, lined with branches and twigs. Cindy paused, there was barely enough space for a duck, never mind an elephant.

Slapper disappeared into the thicket, returning a moment later, "Come on," he said. "How else will you ever know?"

Cindy sniffed the tiny entrance; it smelt peppery and of damp moss. Closing her eyes, she took a deep breath, then another. There was a noise of rustling and snapping of branches, and when she opened them again, the opening had widened. She entered, and as she did her eyes swam in deep pools of uncertainty, drifting over mountains, lakes, and streams. The duck was quacking in some strange language, a language which Cindy didn't understand but yet did.

Suddenly Slapper turned, his face horrid and fierce, fiercer than the fiercest tiger. Cindy's heart jumped, her chest thumped, her tailbone straightened, feathers flew, and eggshells shattered, and her trunk howled a long melancholic note of despair. On they went, the duck again turned; this time, it was Cindy's old friend Plop looking back with tears of sorrow. Again, her heart jumped, her tailbone straightened, and a trumpet call filled the still night air. Slapper raised a wing, and a lightning bolt flashed across the sky, and as he flapped, thunder rattled, and the earth beneath their feet trembled. A deep crevasse opened, and from it emerged a huge burp, then a cough and a manic giggle. Cindy's spirit flew from her chest and shot out of her ears. Outside, it flew around looking for a place to hide, but finding nowhere, it returned straight up her trunk and back into her body.

Again and again, the terror fell upon Cindy, and each time, shells and feathers were lost. But slowly, no matter how shocking, how terrifying, or unexpected event befell upon her, her spirit's reaction paled to nothing. She couldn't remember entering the Royal Palace or striking the bell three times. Slapper was gone, she did not know when or where he went, but he was gone. The Cloak of Destiny was in rags, not a seedpod was left, and only a single unbroken shell had survived.

A maternal warmth enveloped her with a touch she wished would go on forever, but no matter how she tried to hold on it, the feeling faded.

The King of Swing

With her tiny heart beating to the racy rhythm of infatuation, Seward's eyes gripped onto Norris as he made his way towards stage left. With his trademark trip, Billy Blackfoot climbed up onto stage, told a few more funny stories and did an amazing magic trick which involved finding lots of eggs from under his wings. He finished with a saucy joke, which Seward didn't approve of, and with a "That's all folks," he bowed and he too disappeared into the wings. Madame Ostrich scrambled to her feet and clumsily made her way onto the stage. From there she called for the performers to return for a collective bow, then nervously read a prepared speech thanking the King for her visit, and wishing her a long and glorious reign. Once she'd finished, the audience rose and joined Madame Ostrich in giving the King a standing ovation.

Although the applause was tumultuous, it didn't register with Seward, her heart was consumed with yearning. She didn't remember returning to the royal tent, brushing her teeth, or even getting into her bedtime shell.

It was early the following morning when she was awoken by a gentle tap on her shell.

"Your Majesty," It was Cindy. The elephant was peering down at her King, she was holding a single undamaged eggshell. With a cheery, "Your Majesty, after facing my challenges, I have returned. My strength was tested, but I persevered and now I stand before you, ready to protect and serve."

"Returned from where?" replied Seward, her head fuzzy from a night of disturbed sleep.

"From the Palace, Your Majesty. Three times I rang the bell. My fears have left me," Cindy held the eggshell closer, "Here."

Seward stared blankly, her tentacled eyes only half-focused, "An eggshell? Why do you present it to me?"

Cindy tilted her head to get a closer look at Seward. *There was something different about her; she had changed.* "One shell, complete!"

"Yes, one shell complete," Seward repeated. "Were you there last night?"

"Yes."

"What did you think of him?"

"Who, Your Majesty?"

Seward squinted, her eyes searching Cindy up and down.

Once again, Cindy presented the shell.

Seward's gaze flickered between Cindy and the shell, her mind trying to make sense of the situation. She reached out and touched the smooth surface, its touch brought a sense of familiarity, a fragment of a forgotten memory reawakened.

"Your Majesty," Cindy's eyes twinkled with a new found confidence as she spoke, "This eggshell represents resilience and transformation. It is a symbol of rebirth and renewal. Like a newborn chick, I emerged from my challenge stronger and more determined than ever."

"Tell me," Seward's tone was laced with insecurity.

Cindy leant forward.

Seward was trembling; "What of his connection to Madame Ostrich? Is that what you discovered?"

Cindy replied, "Madame Ostrich?"

"Yes, the Ostrich." The emotion of love swirled with intrigue, and with jealous yearning.

*

Tommy and Roly were making their way through the jungle, small talk, chitty chatting whilst looking for an isolated spot.

After a quick check for any eavesdroppers, Tommy began. "Let's say…. I have a friend… actually a friend of an acquaintance. Someone who for a price could eradicate our little mollusc problem." He waited for Roly's reaction, then ran a finger across his neck and winked.

Roly didn't trust Tommy, never mind his so called acquaintance. "No, that might result in a situation none of us wants," he sounded like a pompous parson. "Bare in mind our objective at all times must be for the good of the Kingdom." In reality, his plan was indeed a quick end to Seward, but with Tommy left holding the baby so to speak. "The good of the Kingdom. The good of all!" On they walked, "If we can persuade the King to abdicate, no blood need be spilt." They stopped at a fallen tree trunk. Roly glanced over to his co-conspirator and grinned, "I'm sure I wasn't the only one to notice that the King seemed smitten by that nightingale. The one who sang at the concert."

"Norris!"

"How well do you know that bird?"

"I know all about Norris, The King of Swing Nightingale. Quite a lady's bird, if you catch my drift," Tommy leered.

Roly smiled, "Hear me out. Just a thought, but if we could arrange for Norris… it is Norris you said?"

Tommy nodded.

"Well, if we can arrange for him to perform a very…. private concert for the King, and then if we were to suggest that perhaps the King was…. more than infatuated. She would have crossed the line of a liaison, and have no option but to abdicate."

Tommy liked it; *This racoon is more cunning than I've given him credit for.*

"We must keep everything top secret. Very hush, hush. All we need is evidence that the King and Norris have spent a night together. "Well, Bob's your uncle, Daphne's your aunt, a home run or an act of treason, who cares?"

*

Norris had moved from his old address in a hurry after a clutch of chicks were born with more than a just passing resemblance to our well-known crooner.

He now lived in a hollow of a sycamore tree on Hummingbird Way at the edge of the duck pond.

"Gobble-gobble. Hey-hey!" Tommy called out as he approached.

Norris merrily skipped out, but on recognising Tommy, "Oh, it's you. What do you want?" The nightingale wasn't on perfect terms with the turkey, as Tommy still owed Norris for a concert he'd performed well over a year ago.

"No need to be like that," Tommy extended a friendly wing, "I come with excellent news."

"Just like the last time," said Norris ignoring the outstretched wing, he flew back up to his nest.

"Oh yeah," Tommy reached into his secret pocket and pulled out a large muslin bag of fresh pine seeds. "Sorry, it's taken so long; busy, busy, busy, as they say." He walked over and placed the bag down below Norris' nest.

Norris was taken aback. He was only owed a small bag; this was far more. Although suspicious, he flew down, flipped the edge of the bag open and ducked inside, re-emerging a moment later nibbling on a seed.

It was more of a leer than a smile from Tommy, "I

know I'm late, so a little bit of interest for your trouble, my friend."

Never one to look a gift horse in the mouth, Norris replied, "So what's this all about?"

"A once-in-a-lifetime opportunity my friend. The King has requested a private concert from you tonight in her Royal quarters. What a compliment." He winked, "Just you and the King my friend. Very cozy, very cozy indeed."

Norris decided to play along. He hopped over to his nest, reached inside and pulled out a small red appointment diary. Flipping it open, his beak tracing out each line.

What's he playing at? Tommy stepped closer. Standing over the nightingale he looked down at the Norris' diary. Just a few scratches, the odd footprint, and some grubby stains which looked like worm juice. *Talk about getting too big for your bird's nest.*

Flipping the pages back and forth, Norris looked up, "Looking tight."

Tommy shook his head, and pulled from his pocket another bag of seed, "How tight?"

Norris blew a long whistle, "As it's the King, I'll do it."

"That's wonderful," Tommy said. He slapped his wings together, spat on one and reached out, Norris stretched out his wing, and they shook on it.

"Meet me at the corner of Ostrich Feather Avenue, just before the moon rises above the oak tree. I'll escort you to meet the King." Tommy glanced over both shoulders before discreetly whispering, "Keep it to yourself. All hush hush," he laughed, "We don't want a gaggle of ducks turning up, quacking away ruining things for you.... Oh, and don't mention anything to the dickie birds."

*

Roly was loitering around outside the Royal tent, pretending to be busy checking on the pack animals, but in reality, he was eavesdropping.

Seward and Cindy were talking.

"Test me. Go on test me," Cindy insisted, then without waiting for the King's response, she barked at herself, "Boo!" and then again, "Boo, boo, boo, boo," the last one so loud it shook Seward out of her bed." Cindy smiled, "See Your Majesty, nothing."

But the King was unsure; she had already lined up an elephant called Snuff, and looking forward to a relaxed journey home. She certainly did not want to risk a repeat of the bucking bronco incident she had recently experienced.

"Creep up on me. Throw Something, "suggested Cindy. But when nothing came her way, she called out, "Go on!"

Seward sat back; her head was still fuzzy and unclear. She couldn't be bothered with all this fuss; all she could think about was the sweet song of the nightingale.

Cindy called to one of the servants who was packing away some of the King's attire. "You there. Test me, and you and you." But despite the meerkats best efforts, no one could scare her properly.

The problem was a bit like when you get the hiccups. If you know the scare is coming, well, nothing happens, apart from more hiccupping. It needed to come out of the blue for a proper scare.... "WHAAAA!"

Seward couldn't face anymore of Cindy's nonsense, she dismissed her, then curled inside her shell. Her heart was sick, she needed to be alone.

*

Cindy set off into the jungle in a huff. If the King wouldn't test her, she'd test herself. But that afternoon the jungle was tranquil, with nothing but gentle birdsong and the odd tweet, which wouldn't scare anyone. The only thing that came close was an unexpected splash of cold water from a banana leaf that landed on Cindy's back, making her tail stick out. But that didn't count, *It wasn't a scare, just a natural reaction.* After hours of wandering, she sat down to ponder. Just then, an idea came to her: what if she tested herself by staying out all night?

You may not be aware that an elephant's eyesight is not good at night, and that they are very scared of the dark, particularly when they are on their own. For Cindy to stay out all night, whilst not being unique, would be an achievement. Not bomb-proof, but in that ballpark.

*

Word had gotten around via those pesky dickie birds, *"The King is in love. The King is heartbroken."*

Idle gossip was the last thing Roly wanted to hear, especially if it involved his plan. But then a thought came to him. *What if Norris serenaded Seward from outside the Royal Tent? The King would be drawn like a moth to a flame. Questions would be asked of course. What was the King doing before she was attacked?* He could hear the chorus now. *"What! She was out alone at night! Alone at night? Well, if that's the case, she's only herself to blame."* Tears would be *spilt. Recommendations will need to be made.* Roly chuckled to himself.

On the corner of Ostrich Feather Avenue, Norris was waiting and wondering what the heck he'd got himself into. The turkey was late, at least an hour. Norris hopped up onto a branch and began whistling a tune to pass the time. Soon, an audience of adoring female birds gathered, enraptured by The King of Swing. He was on his third song when Tommy turned the corner.

"What the blazes is going on?" Tommy gobbled furiously, as the smitten females scattered into the darkness. "What are you doing squawking up the neighbourhood?" Shaking his head in disbelief, "I told you to keep this to yourself."

Norris didn't like the turkey's attitude, *and for two farthings….* but he was frightened of Tommy, so flew down.

Tommy Turkey looked at him squarely, "We've got business to do." Then by way of an insult added, "Not everyone can lead your life of frivolity and foolishness."

Norris held his beak as under Tommy's wing he noticed another large bag of seed.

"Once the job is done," said Tommy tapping the side of the bag.

The change of plan sounded fine to Norris. In fact, as a nightingale he preferred performing under the stars. They had just turned into Kookaburra Avenue when Roly popped out from behind a bush, shushed them and beckoned them forward. With all three now hiding, they waited, watching, and a bit more watching, making sure they weren't being followed.

With loud crash; Cindy came bursting through the undergrowth, aimlessly throwing dirt onto her back.

"What's she doing?" Roly whispered, as Cindy crossed over Kookaburra Avenue and disappeared again into the jungle.

Confused, Tommy shrugged, "I... I thought elephants didn't go out alone at night.

Norris was about to comment, but Tommy muffled him under his wing.

There they stayed huddled together, until the sound of breaking branches faded into the distance.

Roly drummed his claws against the side of his head; *The elephant could scupper the plan.* A hoot of an owl made him look up, the owl blinked, looked down at the conspirators and hooted three times. It was a feeling; something didn't seem right. His mind was adrift, what had he got himself into? He'd always considered himself loyal, a good servant, maybe....

But with the plan now in implementation, he wasn't sure. Tommy was whispering in Norris' ear. What if the two of them have worked something out? He didn't trust the turkey, not one bit, and as for Norris, well, if ever there was a perfect example of a birdbrain….

Noticing his concern, "What's wrong?" asked Tommy. "The elephant is miles away; we're clear."

Roly bit his bottom lip, "Is there some other way?"

Tommy looked bewildered, "Another way? Another way….? He shook his head, remember, you're the one we're doing this for. You'll be King." Although trying appear restrained, Tommy wattle was beetroot red, ripe and looked ready to burst. "If you can't…. If you can't…" He was ready to blow and let the racoon have both barrels, but held back, this was not the time. No, he must keep a cool head. *Calm yourself, calm yourself. He'll know soon enough this is Bird Land, and what happens here is turkey business. A King killer. As good as dead meat, and to the victor, the spoils.* Tommy spoke reassuringly, "We're all nervous, it's only natural. But remind yourself, this isn't about you or me; it is for the good of the Kingdom. I have nothing personal against the snail, I'm sure he's a perfectly decent fellow, but we have work to do. All we need to do is relax and concentrate on the plan."

"Concentrate on the plan," repeated Norris to no one in particular.

Tommy grinned, "See, concentrate on the plan."

Norris nodded; although he didn't know why.

Within minutes they had found their way to the edge of Seward's camp. With a gobble from Tommy, Norris hopped onto a branch to get himself ready, whilst the other two found a secluded spot from where they could observe. Once the nightingale had settled, Tommy waved a wing. Norris nodded and merrily waved back. Tommy waved again, this time with vigorous intent.

Confused, Norris mouthed, "Now?"

Tommy gobbled out, "Now!"

The nightingale cleared his throat, bowed to the darkened sky and began to sing. His song started with a gentle tremolo woven with overtones of vibrato, the volume wavering back and forth in tender tones. Like a thief, it crept through the night air finding its way through a small opening in the King's tent. It passed by the sleeping servants, the dozy guards and on into Seward's quarters. It hung in the air for a while, contemplating the treachery it was sent to perform, before descending and caressing Seward's shell. The beauty of the song knew its task, passing through her soft body it entered her soul, drifting past her longings and sorrows. It dallied at the emotion of love, then washed over her.

One love-smitten eye opened; Seward was neither asleep nor conscious; she was floating in a world without a care. Whatever she was, she was no more.

All-consuming love, take my body, heart, and soul; let us be one with this mystery.

Norris was skipping along his perch, his song dancing in gleeful mischief.

Tommy nudged Roly and grinned as a glint of light appeared in the tent's entrance.

At first only her tiny head appeared, then slowly her body emerged, it was Seward. Whether she was aware or not, even she didn't know. The moonlight reflected off her shell as she slithered forward, her eyes searching, her heart dragging her towards her doom.

Tommy rubbed his wings together. "Like taking crumbs from a day-old chick." With the swiftness of a predator, he hopped from where he was lurking, sharpening his spurs with every step. After a few steps he was standing over her. Seward's eyes were open but were blind, her neck stretched forward as though offering it to her executioner. Tommy raised his spur, emotion getting the better of him, as from foot to foot, he hopped, contemplating what angle to strike. *A right swish, or perhaps a left swoosh*? He was naturally a southpaw, so the left it was.

With a swoosh of slicing flesh, the beautiful song suddenly ended as Norris tweeted in panic at the flailing body lying in the dust. But it was not Seward who was gasping her last breath, but that of that cruel assassin Tommy Turkey. Standing over him was Roly, his claw wet with the turkey's blood. Norris didn't need to be told and with an anxious flutter, he disappeared into the night.

"Your Majesty, Your Majesty, please wake." Roly was gently tapping Seward's shell.

The stalks of her eyes tried to focus. Groggily, she responded, "What am I doing here?"

"Let me get you inside," said Roly, then called out for help.

Once safely inside and with servants fussing and running this way and that, Roly explained to Seward his version of the truth.

"Your Majesty, with all that has been going on," he shook his head, "No, I must speak candidly." Roly took a deep breath, "Your Majesty, thoughts have been troubling me since my trial. I cannot explain my distress since that horrendous accusation was made. I have not eaten and hardly slept; it has been awful. Tonight, as I drifted between sleep and consciousness, I heard something strange; birdsong, so bewitching that I thought it was part of a dream. I doubted myself. But the more I listened it became apparent the song was not inside my head, it was coming from outside the Royal Caravan. I went out to investigate, the song was now louder, enchanting, captivating, I could not help but follow its call. It was then that I spotted you, Your Majesty, and to my horror I also saw Tommy Turkey hovering over you ready to strike." Roly swallowed back a tear before saying, "It could have ended…." his words trailed off as though the thought was too troubling, "In…. In…." Roly gripped his chest; it was all too much.

There was a sharp trumpet call, "Let me through. Let me through." Cindy brushed past the guards who were blocking her way. She knelt on one knee. "My Liege."

Roly suddenly forgot about his heart attack, scrambled to his feet, and also got down on one knee. "At your service, Your Majesty."

Seward was sleepy; she dismissed the pair and returned to bed. Yet despite her exhaustion she could not settle; the haunting song of the nightingale had not finished with her.

In that place between reality and the stars, whispers came to her, whispers of isolation and despair. Norris was nearby, gracefully tending to his feathers, a picture of elegance and charm. He drew closer. Seward's eyes lingered, then drifted.

"Can you see the beauty?" she whispered; her voice barely audible. "Sing to me, little sparrow."

Norris cleared his throat and, tapping his foot, began searching for a rhythm. A couple of slightly off-key chirps escaped. Seward smiled reassuringly, encouraging him to continue. He again cleared his throat.

"Little sparrow, sing to me."

Norris took a deep breath and sang a song that glided and trickled over her. But his song was covered in a darkness that consumed everything.

Her head swayed gently to and fro, her mind in a land long since forgotten. Visions flickered; the boundaries of time blurred, the future and the past mingled and twisted. There was her old friend Plop. She glimpsed Roly, and even the diabolical Tommy Turkey. Dead bodies were surrounded by vultures snarling, snapping, tearing.

She looked to him, her eyes soft, her breath slow. Who was he, where had he come from, was he angel or devil? "Another song, my little sparrow."

Roly on a Knife Edge

The morning arrived all too soon. Seward groggily peeked out of her shell.

Cindy was standing by her side, chest puffed out, trunk up in a sharp right-angled salute, "Good morning, Your Majesty."

Seward blinked and let out the tiniest of grunts, "What time is it?"

Cindy did her usual thing of counting back from some event or other, then frustratedly called to one of the servants, "What time is it?"

"Breakfast time!" said a cheeky-faced meerkat carrying a ripe strawberry on a purple cushion.

"Breakfast time," Cindy repeated.

Seward wasn't hungry and dismissed the servant. She looked up at Cindy for some sort of recognition or alarm. But just a doleful stare.

After what seemed like an age, Cindy spoke, "I've put the raccoon into custody, Your Majesty."

But surely Roly had saved her? Seward stretched herself to present as imposing a figure as she could muster. "Why....?" And without waiting for an answer, "Release the raccoon immediately."

"But Your Majesty."

Seward squeezed another fraction from her tiny frame, "Immediately! And bring him to me."

Cindy looked puzzled and was about to speak, but fearing her position, she followed the King's command.

Suddenly from outside came frantic sounds of gobbling. It was Agnes Turkey flapping her wings and pecking at all and sundry, "Where is my husband? Where have you got him?" Each gobble louder and more vulgar than the one before.

"Get her out of here," said Cindy. "Your husband was nothing more than an assassin. He got what he deserved."

"But I have a brood to feed. Who's going to help me?" More disgusting gobbles, more crashing, "Let me see the King."

"Get out, get out," Cindy trumpeted. "He should have thought of you, before."

The anguished gobbles of Agnes got quieter and more distant as she was led away.

Although I have not mentioned Tommy Turkey's wife Agnes that often. They'd actually been married for over five years with a family of twenty-five of grown-up turkeys, and a clutch of eggs ready to hatch. Tommy would have insisted differently, but in Bird Land, it was said to be hen pecked. I couldn't say that was completely true, but their relationship was strong. Agnes had been a good wife to Tommy, a little short tempered, yes, but fiercely loyal.

*

Roly was led by Madame Ostrich, Chief of the Council of Bird Land, through a throng of animals into the Kings Quarters. He was bound with heavy chains on his legs and wrists.

"Release him," Seward shouted as fiercely as she could muster. "Why is he in chains?"

Madame Ostrich was about to answer but Seward's scowl tightened her beak.

Seward's problem was that she had only experienced a certain truth, and as we all know, truth has many faces. She wasn't aware that despite Tommy Turkey's warning, Norris had indeed mentioned the devious plot to the dickie birds, who had told it to the pigeons, who in turn told the ducks, who in the strictest confidence revealed it to the hens. Then the parrots got to hear on a strictly hush-hush basis. By morning, the news of the previous night's events was all over Bird Land.

Roly threw himself prostrate to the ground; claws clasped above his head.

Seward was too tired for his theatrics, "Please. Please, get to your feet."

Roly slowly got up.

"Speak to me," said Seward.

"Your Majesty," Roly bowed, "Your loyal servant."

"We'll see!" Seward glanced up, "Enlighten me?"

Roly admitted there had been a conspiracy so dastardly that it threatened the life of the King. Without wanting to alarm Seward, he'd taken it upon himself to infiltrate the plot and expose Tommy Turkey for the evil traitor he was. "My interest at all times was your safety, Your Majesty."

Seward questioned and probed the racoon further, and whilst not fully believing her former advisor, she could, without doubt, follow his reasoning. By midday, she had heard enough and needed to rest.

Roly was put under house arrest, chained up in the corner of her quarters as Seward took her nap.

After lunching on a buttercup and feeling refreshed, Seward called for Cindy. The elephant bustled forward soldier-like and told a very different story to Roly's. Madame Ostrich's statement completely upset the raccoon's applecart, so to speak, when she declared the plot was indeed the idea of Tommy Turkey's, but Roly had been pleased to go along with it, and that he'd even been promised the crown. Other witnesses were called, dickie birds, pigeons, ducks, hens and parrots. Each of them condemned Roly as a co-conspirator.

Seward was still unsure. *If the birds were all correct and Roly was part of the conspiracy, and as portrayed, his ambitions were indeed above his station, why would he not have allowed that dastardly turkey to complete his mission?* Seward put this to both Madame Ostrich and Cindy, and despite a lot of awkward huffing and puffing from the pair, neither could answer her questions.

Roly's eyes widened, *Perhaps, just perhaps.*

"Two and two make four," called out a parrot. "Two and two make four," it repeated. There was a pause before the same parrot squawked, "Five and five make fifty-five."

"Get that bird out of here," shouted Seward, then, "Where is the nightingale?"

Madame Ostrich's head popped out of the dust and scanned 360 degrees.

"Don't you think we need evidence from the nightingale?" asked Seward.

Cindy blasted out a trumpet call, "Find the nightingale." There was a rush of elephants and every bird you could imagine, off in search of Norris.

"Find the nightingale," Roly called out.

Cindy told him to shut up, "A traitors' advice is never welcome."

Roly was shuffling around trying to get comfortable, but no matter what, he just couldn't settle. A thought came to Seward; she would count the times Roly switched his position, and her decision on whether he lived or died would pivot on it. If it was an even number by nightfall, Roly would be pardoned; but if it was odd, Roly fate would be sealed. By the middle of the afternoon, Roly had shifted position precisely fifty times. By evening the number was seventy-two, which happened to be the King's lucky number. Seward had been thinking of changing her lucky number; seventy-two hadn't proved its worth. She was contemplating between seventy-five and seventy-eight and after meandering between the two she settled on seventy-five, then realised she'd lost count of Roly's position changes. "Dash it to hell," she called out, inventing the first Royal curse words.

Cindy looked up, "I beg your pardon, Your Majesty?"

"Dash it to hell," Seward repeated.

Cindy looked even more puzzled, "D…"

"I've lost count," screamed Seward in her tiny voice.

"Ah, let me help you," offered Cindy, " What number were you on?"

Their conversation roused Roly, and he too tried helping. "What number were you on?"

"Never you mind," said Seward curtly.

"I think a fright might help," suggested Cindy.

"That's for hiccups, stupid," said Roly. "You need to remember what number you were on and your thoughts at the time. Simply retrace your steps. It always helps me. Or keep count using your whiskers…" Then realising Seward's apparent lack in the whisker department, he trailed off.

Seward tried retracing her thoughts, but with the distraction of Cindy and Roly arguing, it was no good. The more she tried, the more difficult it became until she couldn't remember why she was counting anyway.

Cindy blurted out, "One hundred," hoping to get lucky, but with no response, she ventured, "Five hundred." She was about to offer fifty-seven when a withering glance from Seward shut her down.

Roly shook his head in disgust, *Stupid animal.*

There was a kerfuffle at the entrance as Madam Ostrich made her way through, "The fugitive has been detained."

Seward's heart skipped and tapped a longing beat in her tiny chest. Of course, she wanted to get to the bottom of the plot, but it broke her heart that Norris was involved. "Where?" *Just once more to hear his sweet song.*

"In the deepest part of the jungle, Your Majesty. An eagle spotted the traitor and arrested him."

"Madame Ostrich, everyone is entitled to a hearing in my Kingdom," responded Seward. "By the way, what has happened to the turkey's body? Has it been checked for any evidence?"

Madam Ostrich looked embarrassed, "I'm afraid the vultures got to it, Your Majesty. All that is left is a bag of pine seeds.

"I can help with that, Your Majesty," Roly volunteered, "The seeds were payment to the nightingale."

It was not the news that Seward wanted to hear.

What Evidence

Norris was brought forward, his feathers muddy and in disarray. He certainly didn't look like 'The King of Swing' anymore. Gone was the swagger of gala night, his confidence displaced with fear. Madame Ostrich was pulling him along on a grass-linked chain; on either side were two stout elephants. She pointed to a spot in front of the King. Norris took his position and bowed his head. He stood stoney still, seemingly too frightened to look up.

Madame Ostrich read out the charge.

Seward wanted to call out, "Release him!" but she knew this could not be, well, not until she had at least heard some evidence. She panned across to Roly and quickly changed her mind about the raccoon's possible innocence.

"State your full name," said a looming Madame Ostrich.

"Norris Nightingale," his voice barely a whisper.

"Speak up," demanded Madame Ostrich.

With his voice aquiver, Norris repeated his name.

Seward wanted him to sing to her, for her heart to float again. *Why was life so complicated?*

Madam Ostrich gazed accusingly at Norris, "Can you tell me where you were yesterday evening?"

He mumbled a stutter.

"Speak up," Madame Ostrich repeated.

Norris looked to Seward, "I didn't mean it, Your Majesty. I would never do anything to hurt you."

"That's not answering the question," Madame Ostrich snapped.

At that, Norris broke down into uncontrollable sobs.

Seward spoke, "I think we all know where he was." She sneered in Roly's direction. "I'm pretty sure that's already been established."

A little confused by the interruption, Madame Ostrich waited a few moments before going on, "Now that we've established that, please elucidate for us why you were outside the King's tent?" The Ostrich was enjoying herself, her manner a blend of haughty theatre and plain simple showing off.

Norris explained that Tommy Turkey had approached

him to perform a private concert for the King. He bowed to Seward, "The thought of singing solely to you Your Majesty was beyond my wildest dreams. So of course I accepted."

Madame Ostrich waved a wing, "Did you not consider this strange? After all, anything of that importance would be delivered through the proper channels." With an aristocratic glare she scanned her audience, confirming to all present that it was she who was the 'proper channels'.

"In hindsight, yes. I should have asked more questions. In future, I'll make sure that requests were received through the proper channels." Norris nodded in the ostrich's direction.

Madame Ostrich raised the tip of her beak just that bit higher, smiled graciously and bowed to the King.

Seward smiled approvingly.

With a look in his eye, which all took for sincerity, Norris went on to say that never in a million years did he think that Tommy and Roly had treachery in mind. He explained that he was halfway through his song when he spotted the King, who seemed to be enjoying the performance. "I certainly enjoyed performing for you, Your Majesty."

Seward's head went coquettishly to one side, her

whole body, including her shell, flushed bright red.

Norris went on, "I was coming to the crescendo, when from the corner of my eye, I spotted that dirty… dirty, Tommy Turkey," Norris pretended to spit on the ground, "creeping from his hiding place, razor-sharp spur raised to the King's throat. Without thought of my own safety, I flew at the assassin knocking him off balance and with all my strength I managed to turn his spur on himself. It was then Roly the Raccoon came at me like a crazed animal. We scuffled, and although he was far larger than me, my lightning speed and sheer pluck managed to keep him at bay. Fortunately, the clatter of the melee alerted the guards who came charging forward. Once I saw that the King was safe, I returned to my branch." Norris paused, until the atmosphere was just right, "It was nothing more than any of your loyal servants would have done, Your Majesty," before bowing graciously.

A round of applause rang out.

Norris accepting his plaudits with a humble smile.

Dear reader, I have to be honest and tell you that I've never been a great judge of character, which has been to the detriment of both my heart and my pocket on many occasions. But it now seems evident that Norris the Nightingale was not as stupid as I first thought.

Norris' explanation matched precisely with Seward's thoughts. Tommy and Roly had taken advantage, plundering his innocence for their treacherous plan. Seward stretched up out of her shell, "This is an obvious case of mistaken identity. I command that Norris the Nightingale be released."

Madame Ostrich's eyelashes fluttered. She beckoned the King, "But…but."

"Next case," said Seward with the authority that only a truly great leader could command. As far as she was concerned, it was an open-and-shut case. She cut short Roly's plea for clemency and with a wave of her eyelashes condemned him to death, even adding that as his crime was a treasonable offence, he should be hung, drawn and quartered, and his body flung to the furthest reaches of the Kingdom.

A moment later, to the astounded audience, Seward also announced that the boundaries that divided her Kingdoms were to be scrapped. From now on, there would only be one land, a land that was free and open to all subjects. Then, to top it all, she asked Norris to perform a song by way of celebration. His delivery was pitch-perfect, and sweeter than ever. Seward's heart danced in ecstasy.

Word soon spread that the King had been the victim of a treasonous plot, and to her credit, she'd dealt with it swiftly and decisively, thus establishing herself as a fair and firm leader. Now was the time for stability, and Seward was the snail for the job.

That said, there was a certain consternation about the re-opening of borders; after all, there was an excellent reason they had borders, The Book of Unheavenly Creatures.

But of course, Seward was not thinking straight and couldn't give a fig about some old superstitious book. She was in love, and as we all know, when love enters the room, intellect bows in homage.

Seward and Norris

With Seward's connections Norris was welcomed into courtly life, and he took to it like a duck to water. Day after day both he and Seward could be seen on the Royal Balcony taking breakfast. Then later they would take a gentle stroll through the Pleasure Gardens, sometimes stopping for a snack or an impromptu picnic.

With Norris' help Seward created the Museum of Xum to house the many wonders of the Kingdom. Norris curated, deciding on what to collect, what was culturally significant and was just a fad. He had artistic taste and a very good eye. Without doubt, without Norris' help, the project would never have got off the ground. Seward's favourite specimens were two giant nautilus shells, and although Norris found them inelegant, she insisted they were given pride of place on either side of the museum entrance.

With the amount of time Seward and Norris were spending together, jealous rumours swirled. Norris' character was discussed and questioned. Tommy Turkey's widow Agnes was the most vocal, spreading disgusting gossip about, 'The King of Swing'. When

Seward heard the widow's lies, she gave Mrs Turkey an hour to vacate her nest, take whatever she could carry and leave the Kingdom. A harsh punishment, but at times a King has to act decisively.

What happened next was a complete one-off, never heard of before or since. An old hyena bitch by the name of Tyrra came across Agnes' vacated nest, which had seven unhatched eggs inside. Greedily, Tyrra ate five of them but with her tummy full, she left the other two for later and settled down for a nap. On awakening, she felt something stirring beneath her, and lifting a leg was shocked to see two chicks chirping for all they were worth. Tyrra's first thoughts were to gobble them straight down, but on second thoughts decided to save them for later. So, tucking them back under her leg, she settled down again. After a couple of hours of excellent dozing, Tyrra awoke refreshed. She yawned, got up and stretched. The chicks too were awake and making one hell of a racket as they begged for food. Tyrra stood for a few moments watching them, then went to the nearest puddle for a drink, but after two slurps, she returned to comfort the noisy chicks.

After being thrown out of her clan by the bossy leader, Tyrra the hyena was a loner. She wasn't what you might call pretty, hyenas generally aren't, but she was downright ugly. Half her ears were missing, scars covered her snout, and as she was suffering from some sort of mange, she only had a semblance of fur.

Seeing the hungry open mouths, Tyrra managed to regurgitate some food and watched as the chicks gobbled down the remains of their brothers and sisters without the slightest hint of embarrassment. Tyrra gave them names; the chick who was the loudest, she called Gobby. The other one, who like herself, was forever scratching, she called Scratcher.

We can forget about this unusual family for now, but they will return later in our story.

*

Since being taken under Seward's wing, Norris had become an even bigger star. Hardly a day passed when he wasn't performing to the great and the good. Seward was pleased for him; he could perform wherever, her only request was that he return to the Palace every evening to sing to her at bedtime. This all worked fine until, over breakfast one morning, Norris let slip that he'd been invited to perform for the whales. Although it would be the first-ever performance of a bird in their watery Kingdom, Norris shrugged, saying it was a great compliment but that he couldn't possibly consider it.

Seward smiled, and although not really wanting to,

she insisted he go.

Norris grinned and warbled out a happy tune that melted her heart.

He scoffed and laughed at the idea of an escort of eagles, saying he was a big bird now, he'd be fine travelling alone.

Seward waved him goodbye and watched as he circled the palace twice, then swooping down blew Seward a kiss, and disappeared over the Palace walls. He'd hardly been gone a moment, and already Seward realised how much she missed him. That night she couldn't sleep; *What if he had an accident? Or was attacked?* There was many a creature out there who would make a light snack of a nightingale. *Oh, why wouldn't he agree to an escort?*

But Norris had a secret so huge that if Seward was to find out, at best his days as the King's escort would be over, worst doesn't bare thinking about.

Fours days went by, which doesn't sound a particularly a long time to you or I, but for Seward it seemed like a lifetime. Listless and off her food, she was wasting away. Her shell more of a cave than a comfy fit. Every evening Cindy would trumpet a gentle lullaby, which although was beautiful, it wasn't Norris. Blinky suggested that perhaps she should go on a tour to distract herself. Seward initially agreed and arrangements were made, but on the day she was due to leave, she couldn't find the energy. It was obvious to one and all that she was suffering from a severe case of love sickness.

Then one morning on awakening, there he was perched on the edge of her bed. Norris looked a bit thinner and his feathers had a certain sheen that she had never noticed before, but his eyes looked bright and full.

"Good morning," said Norris, "How is my King this fine morning?"

Seward was so excited that she almost slipped from her shell, "You're back."

Norris cocked his head in the air and sang with all his might,

Good morning my dear

To have you so near

Is like pecking a pear!

It must be said that while Norris could undoubtedly

hold a tune, his lyrical qualities did not match his vocal ability.

"Oh, Norris.... I've missed you.... sooo... much."

"I've missed you too."

Suddenly Norris began flying at a blurring speed back and forth, between the King's bed and the throne. Poor Seward's eyesight couldn't keep up with him. When he finally swooped down and they embraced, her tiny heart almost stopped.

"Look what I have brought you," Norris skipped back and picked up what looked like a reddish-green plant in his beak. It wasn't a flower, and certainly didn't smell like one. He hopped closer and presented it to Seward, "Here taste it."

Hesitantly Seward touched the surface then suddenly pulled back. It tasted pungent and salty, but there was also some other flavour which was new to Seward. After taking a few more nibbles, she smiled, "What is it?"

"It is from the oceans. It's called seaweed. Nice, hey? This is only one type. There are many more, all delicious and very good for the digestive system."

Seward took another bite, "It is delicious!"

"I thought you would like it."

"I love it," Seward beamed.

Whether or not Seward picked up on it, I'm not sure, but Norris' tone had changed imperceivably, but nonetheless, it had changed.

"I will bring you a different one next time."

Seward hadn't considered a next time but was so pleased to see Norris she resisted the temptation to broach the subject. For the rest of the day, they cavorted on the nautilus shells together, and when night approached, Norris sang to her The Secret Song of the Whale, a song so beautiful it made Seward cry.

Cindy had noted how things were going between her King and the nightingale. She couldn't put her trunk on it, but somewhere in the back of her mind.... something wasn't right. No one could fail to be impressed by Norris' bravery in saving the King from certain death or his devotion to her, but there was something.... Cindy decided to keep a closer eye, and it wasn't long when she noticed a strange thing. Not long after nightfall, when Seward was asleep, a small bird would perch on the outer walls of the Palace and sing, and from deep inside the Royal quarters would come a reply. Probably all innocent, but…

For a while, Seward had been mulling things over.

When she mentioned her thoughts to Norris, his eyes lit up, and he sang a song in delight. Of course, arrangements would have to be made, invitations sent, this sort of thing couldn't be organised at the drop of a hat.

With a slimy ring around the date Seward marked her calendar. The wedding was to be in two weeks, and to celebrate the event, a three-day holiday for all of the Kingdom. There would be festivities, starting early and ending late, with a special concert which Norris would head up. The invitations read:

Everyone is officially invited to the forthcoming wedding of the King to her beloved Norris the Nightingale.

The event will take place at the Palace of Xum.

All will be expected to be presented at their best.

Any creature found to be scruffy or dirty will be turned away.

By Order

King Seward

P.S. Norris, The King of Swing, will be performing.

Cindy gently voiced her concerns, saying that perhaps Seward was rushing into things. After all, she had only known Norris for a short while.

"Fiddlesticks!" Seward replied. "Do you think your King does not know the right time for 'one' to marry?"

"I do not doubt that, Your Majesty. But perhaps.... It's just that something has come to my attention. It will only take me a day or two." Cindy paused, "Probably nothing, but I think we should be.... cautious."

Seward's response was abrupt, "Fiddlesticks! If you value your position, you'll do as I command."

And as Cindy did value her position, "As you wish, Your Majesty," she bowed and left.

With so many invitations, barely a banana leaf was left in the jungle. The gorillas made their thoughts clear; the cull would risk the crop. Whilst sympathetic, Cindy explained that her trunk was tied, and that the banana leaf invitations were by royal command.

Sorry to keep butting in, but here's another little fact you may or may not know. It was gorillas who first invented umbrellas. I know they say it was the

Chinese, but that's not true; gorillas were definitely first, using banana leaves, simple but effective. There is also a theory that sending out the invitations forced your first basic humans out of the canopy in search of food. It's only a theory, but if you ask me???

On the day of the wedding, there was a buzz around the Palace that had not been seen since Sammy the Skunk King organised the Great Stink Carnival.

Seward was in her Royal quarters being fussed over by her servants and a pair of butterflies; dressmakers renowned for their excellent taste.

Norris was on his perch. He couldn't believe his luck. To have come from lowly crooner to become the Kings consort, well if you didn't know better, you'd think it was something taken from a fairy tale. He was in a separate wing of the Palace and had employed a kingfisher as his sartorial advisor. To cover his dull brown colour, the kingfisher chose a cloak of peacock feathers, which shimmered like a waterfall as he moved. He wore a headdress of gold bougainvillaea, and around his ankles were bangles of tiny red verbena. His best man was Charlie the Crow, a rather dull, colourless character; the less said the better.

Queues were tailing back for miles were forming outside the Palace as the beavers, acting as security, thoroughly checked everyone's appearance and invitation. In an effort to get in quicker, some guests began jostling and pushing, but they weren't going nowhere. The diligent beavers weren't going to be rushed.

Meercats had been busy since dawn preparing the food in the kitchens. For her special day, Seward had chosen a menu of seven varieties of seaweed along with duck eggs and shrimp. Not everyone's taste, but when has the food at a wedding party ever been. Squabbling penguins, who were acting as waiters for the day, were getting ready the liquid refreshments, either fresh, salt or muddy water, the selection.

Seward had waived off Norris' idea of a formal dinner and decided instead on a garden party. After the wedding ceremony, the entertainment would include three concerts, firstly one by the blackbirds, then sparrows and skylarks. Also performing were Scott the Tarantula, a magician from Insect Land, an antelope act called the Vixen Flyers with their highwire act. A comedy troupe of dogs and chimpanzees would provide the laughs, and then of course, the finale, Norris the King of Swing.

By the middle of the morning, the place was alive with grunts, buzzes, barks, roars, bellows, birdsong, and chatter of every animal sound you can imagine, as well as quite a few you couldn't.

A sharp fanfare of trumpets rang out, guests stopped what they were doing, and looked toward the Royal quarters. A hush descended. Another flurry of trumpets sounded, and the unicorns Harold and Berti stepped out leading a procession of swans towards an altar of vines and rose petals. A screech or scream of a peacock's call signalled a flock of yellow and green parrots flying forward in pairs. Norris was flying behind and behind him, the best man. The parrots split, leaving Norris and the crow to perch before the altar.

The minister was a hearty-looking octopus renowned for his gentle humour. He reached out a welcoming tentacle and with a warm smile, "Great day for it," glancing up at the cloudless sky, "We couldn't ask for a better one."

Norris brusquely nodded, then stood in stony silence alongside Charlie the Crow. Five minutes passed, and before you knew it, half an hour had gone. Norris was getting nervous, shuffling back and forth and continuously glancing over his shoulder.

But Seward was never one to hurry, least of all for her own wedding. He could shuffle as much as he wanted; it wouldn't make the slightest difference.

"What's keeping her?" Norris pecked at Charlie.

Charlie didn't respond.

With a warm chuckle, the minister smiled, "It would be a sad world if the King couldn't be late for her own wedding." Then leaning towards Norris, "All things come to those who wait."

Norris glanced over his shoulder and straightened a loose feather, his mind was racing. Time passed, and so did the sun, which was now creeping back down through the sky.

"Where is she?" Norris blurted, then immediately regretted his words.

The minister offered, "Don't worry, I'm sure everything is alright."

But the minister's words didn't help Norris, as when panic consumes us, reassurance is rarely helpful.

Seward had no idea of the time; she was having great fun trying on outfits. First, a two-piece suit made of golden leaves. Next, she tried on a gown of silk, laced with splinters of crystal. It looked great but was very uncomfortable. She pulled on a sleek dress made of rose petals, it showed off her figure to a treat, and after a glance into Cindy's eye, which she was using as a mirror, she took a deep breath and announced that she was ready.

A hum filtered through the air as elephants blew on the nautilus shells. The sound grew, filling the Palaces and on out into the Kingdom. There was something about the low-frequency sound, which felt unnerving, but then came a calmness. Even Norris relaxed, his nervous tick a distant memory.

A team of elephants stepped forward in unison, thundered a hypnotic boom, boom, boom.

Cindy appeared; she was robed in a lace cloak made from a billion spider webs with yellow lilies. On her head was seated Seward, a picture of beauty, poise and elegance. They slowly made their way around the interior of the Palace.

Norris began singing;

Here comes the bride

She slips but never slides

We'll share an apple pie

But never a bumblebee…

And that was it; he didn't go on.

Guests looked at each other, scratching their heads. Some began to giggle as Norris took a bow.

When Cindy arrived at the altar two dragonflies swooped down and picked up Seward, gently lowering her beside her bridegroom. Norris glanced over; Charlie the Crow bent forward for a good ogle before receiving a jealous peck from Norris to straighten him up.

"Let me say, Your Majesty, you look delightful," said the minister.

Seward smiled, her eyelashes fluttered, and she blushed a shade of green.

Embarrassed, the minister coughed, wiped his forehead, glanced at Norris, and nodded apologetically. Raising his tentacles, he reached out to his flock. "Creatures of the Kingdom... We are gathered here today to witness the wedding of King Seward..." he glanced at his notes, "to... Norris, The King of Swing."

The minister proceeded to bore everyone going on at length about the sanctity of marriage and the need for more love in the Kingdom. He told a long winded story about a fish that saved a fish from another fish and then a story about a dying hedgehog's last wish, blah, blah, blah.

The congregation began mumbling and whispering to each other. The once joyful energy was dropping as quickly as a stone thrown down a well.

The minister coughed, checked his notes, then raised his voice, "If any creature should have any objection to this union... Speak now or forever hold... your peace."

There was a hushed silence; Seward glanced at Norris and smiled; he blew a romantic kiss.

Then it began. A nervous quack, then another quack, followed by a tweet, a chirp, a hoot, a caw, a tiny trill, and finally a croak, as a pretty little frog hopped forward.

You could have heard a feather drop.

So, you see, my friends, Norris' secret was that he was not only a wanton liar but also a serial bigamist.

In the hope of rushing proceeding along, Norris grabbed at his Seward, she pulled back. He tried again. This time Seward swooned.

Creatures surged forward, lions were snarling, crocodiles snapping, and bulls charging. Cries of, "Bigamist! Traitor! Get him!" were heard as the nightingale dashed for cover.

Just as it seemed Norris' chances were slim to none, with a skip and a hop, he was in the air, higher and higher he went, and in the confusion, Norris was gone.

Cindy lifted Seward and returned her to her quarters.

From the start, Cindy knew Norris was a wrong un, but even in her wildest dreams, she hadn't considered that he'd was married eight times, and still was.

When she awoke, Seward asked what had become of Norris.

"He's gone, Your Majesty; we've sent out a search party. But as yet...." Cindy shook her head consolingly, stepped back and saluted, "I'll await your instructions."

"Can you bring him to me? Please bring him back to me."

Cindy smiled, "I will try."

There and then, Cindy decided whether alive or dead, Norris would never be found, she would make sure of it.

The Return of the Turkey

Deep in the jungle two young turkeys awoke from their afternoon naps.

Gobby had now outgrown his sister. He had large clawed feet, thick black feathers, and a red wattle, but was somewhat dim-witted. The brains of the family went to his sister Scratcher, who was much lighter in colour, with keen eyes and strong opinions.

As they got older Tyrra explained how she had found them alone in an empty nest, but omitted the demise of their possible brothers and sisters. She told them of the banishment of their mother and the cruel end of their father Tommy Turkey. At the age they were neither Gobby or Scratcher were that interested, as far as they were concerned Tyrra the hyena was their mother, as it was her who fed, protected, and cared for them.

Tyrra's clutch were not regular turkeys however, pecking for seeds and worms. No, she had raised them to be fearsome, flesh-eating turkeys, as cunning as any hyena. She'd taught them the tricks of the trade, so to speak. So, when on a hunt, you tease your prey, linger, confuse, intrigue and entertain whilst all the time getting closer. If you are still, often your dinner will come to you. Rabbits are suckers for flattery, and to steer clear of foxes.

"Hey, what's the plan today?" Gobby asked no one in particular, nudging a bone.

Tyrra looked up momentarily, gazed at her son, then went back to licking the wound she'd received from the boar she'd killed during the night.

Scratcher stuck her beak into the air and sniffed, she looked to her mother.

Tyrra nodded.

"See how I got hold of him by the snout," Gobby was flapping his wings as he gripped onto a remnant of the boar's cheek. "I bet he'd never dealt with anyone like me before." He dropped the morsel, pecked at it again and strutted over to his sister. "Breakfast is served."

Scratcher ignored the gift and hopped alongside Tyrra.

"We'll go higher," said the hyena. "They prefer lowland."

"Who do?" Gobby looked over.

Scratcher raised her beak, "Lions, stupid."

Gobby sniffed, but was oblivious to the pungent odour in the air, "I can't smell lions."

"Wash your face," his mother called.

Gobby remembered his first encounter with lions when he was learning how to hunt deer. Tyrra his mother was surveying a small herd and had picked out a fawn to kill. Just as she was about to attack, a lone male buffalo wandered by, muscular, jet black with fearsome horns. When out from nowhere two female lions charged, one clamped its jaws onto the buffalo's face, the other leapt on its back. The buffalo twisted, turned, kicked and bellowed, but couldn't shake them off. Eventually exhausted the buffalo fell to its knees. Gobby was transfixed. But death did not come quick, it could have been hours, but in reality, it was only minutes the animal struggled. Then with eyes bulging like bloodshot moons, the buffalo somehow managed to heave itself upright and turning quickly and gored one of the lions, the other one too. They let go, but as the weary buffalo made its escape it slipped, and when a one-eyed male lion joined the fray, the buffalo's brave fight for life was truly over. Gobby was enthralled both with fear and exhilaration. He remembered asking his mother if he could grow up to be a lion? Tyrra threw back her head, laughing as she had never laughed before.

There it was a roar, Tyrra's ears pricked up. Then another, deeper, stronger. The lions were closing in. Leaving the remains of their kill behind, Tyrra, Scratcher and Gobby moved quickly over the savanna until the roars faded into the distance.

As the day drifted towards evening Tyrra spotted a cave where they could rest. Followed by Scratcher and Gobby, she cautiously entered. It was clear apart from remnants of bones, dried poo and discarded nests. "This will do us for now," said Tyrra as she sniffed the ground.

Scratcher was about to say something when through the darkness she caught sight of a moving figure and let out a warning gobble.

The black figure rose and made a sound, something between a shriek and a yelp. Behind the creature were its young, small bundles of fur, huddled, fearfully watching as their mother took a stance and shook herself, ready to fight.

Tyrra immediately recognised the beast as a bear. Today we'd call them sloth bears, but for Tyrra, all bears were the same and not to be tangled with.

The foolhardy Gobby began circling forward, the bear swung out a paw. Gobby nimbly skipped back and moved to the right, then leapt at the bear pecking at her ear. Tyrra saw her chance; slipping behind she sank her teeth into the furry rump. The bear spun, and pinned Tyrra to the floor, then began ripping into her flesh. In Tyrra's defence Gobby now aimed his pecks at the bear's eyes, but a vicious swing of her head sent him tumbling unconscious into a dim corner of the cave. With a grunt, the bear let go of Tyrra, then turned and followed +Gobby into the darkness.

Scratcher wanted to rescue her brother, but Tyrra knew it was useless, they had to get out of the cave, or they, too, would die at the paws of the terrible beast. Scrambling outside, they took refuge behind a rock. As Tyrra licked at a gaping would in her belly, Scratcher climbed on top of the rock.

The bear appeared at the entrance of the cave, Gobby's lifeless body in her jaws. She flung him onto the ground, then began plucking his feathers with her teeth. Her cubs padded forward, huddling beside their mother and hungrily sniffing at the corpse.

To add to their troubles once again came the roar of lions. They were heading in their direction. Tyrra was losing a lot of blood, but they had to go. Scratcher helped her mother to her feet.

It was by the side of a stream that Tyrra spoke her last words, words so shallow they were barely audible, "Fight for what is yours."

Scratcher raised her head and let out a forlorn gobble. It was a day of sorrow, but she was a warrior, a survivor, a turkey.

Scratcher's Rise

If her ambition was to be matched by deeds, Scratcher realised that her knowledge was limited. So, for the years, three months and three days she wandered throughout the Kingdom of Xum. She discovered the cruelty of the jungle, the patience of the desert, the guile of the savanna and the wisdom of the seas. When she was ready, she chose a mate, it wasn't love or even friendship, it was the start of a dynasty.

Scratcher built her nest overlooking the Palace. A month later her first chicks hatched, a male and a female. She called the male Turvey, as he reminded her of her brother Gobby, dim, but very brave. Turvey was black from the tip of his beak to the end of his tail, with a wattle; which almost draped on the ground. The female had a twisted beak which not line up. Instead of chirping like any normal chick, she lisped, or perhaps better described as a whistle. So that's what Scratcher called her, Whistle. Whistle's feathers were white apart from her dark eyebrows.

To protect herself and her brood Scratcher created a kind of fort or compound. It was made from stones, mud, twigs, bones, basically anything she could get her wings on, and called it, Tip Top Turkey Trot. It wasn't a particularly nice place, in fact, it was filthy and dirty, with feathers and turkey faeces everywhere. Still, Scratcher wanted it rough, the rougher the better as far as she was concerned. She wanted tough turkey warriors, not soft chickens.

Every day when Scratcher would leave her chicks to hunt, returning at night to feed and entertain her brood with a story. It was from a two-thousand-year-old tortoise, or so it said, that Scratcher had learnt the art of storytelling. Like the tortoise she would add more than just a sprinkling of embellishment.

Turvey and Whistle believed that their eggshells were purple. That it was a mollusc who built the Palace of Xum to separate the elite from the rest of the animals. They believed that the Snail King was a usurper, and it was Scratcher's father, Tommy Turkey, grandson of Tony the Magnificent who should have been King.

"Mark my words, my darlings. We turkeys will have our day."

It is in the innocent that dark seeds of hate thrive.

Turkeys are magnificent breeders, and it wasn't long before Scratcher's small flock expanded to eighteen, then forty-eight, and with another clutch of eggs on the nest, it would soon be one hundred and two.

Scratcher taught her brood the life lessons that Tyrra had taught her. These turkeys were strictly carnivores and worked as a pack, each vicious, mean and cunning, and capable of bringing down animals much bigger than themselves. Even lions and tigers kept out of their way.

It was essential to Scratcher that her flock followed an ethos, otherwise known as, The code of Tip Top Turkey Trot. So once a week all would gather by the centre perch, known as the Holy Branch of Gobble. Whistle would whistle the Gospel of Mother Scratcher. It never wavered or changed, simply put, it preached that Turkeys were the true nobility of the Kingdom, the Snail King was a usurper, and their day would come.

On this particular occasion after Whistle had finished, Scratcher stepped forward and hopped up onto the Holy Branch. "My family," she paused and took a weary breath.

"I had a vision last night.

A vision that both alarmed…. and inspired me.

I saw the truth.

A truth of hope

A truth of prayer

Of why we toil.

A truth of why we shed our blood and feathers.

But not a truth that the usurper would agree to."

Scratcher slowly shook her head.

"No! This usurper will never let us live in peace

She is a power-hungry devil who is planning… our destruction."

Whistle whistled, and applauded.

Scratcher went on, "Whether it is today, the next day, the next week or even next year, as sure as Tyrra is my mother, the usurper will invade. She plans to destroy all we've worked for."

Her voice moved up an octave.

"But if that… that…. snail thinks we will roll over! Then she needs to think again." Scratcher arrogantly chuckled, her beak glinted as she shook her head. "War!!! they don't know the meaning of it." She looked down at her flock, her gaze settled on each and every turkey present, testing, probing. "This I can promise you…. I promise, we turkeys will… be Victorious!!!" "We will not wait for that thief, that devil, that fraud! From this day forth, we are at war!"

The energy exploded into a chorus of vigorous gobbles. Every turkey present was up for a scrap and ready to go, but Scratcher knew what she was doing; the time needed to be right. She placed her wing across her breast.

Whistle hopped up alongside her mother and she began a prayer.

"Oh, Mother Sw…cratcher

A heart s'so brave

Of noble th'tought and even hand

To you, we pray of our toil

Oh, Mother Sw…scratcher

S'so Noble, kind and wise

Your wisdom ss'saves us'ss

Oh, Mother Sw…scratcher

With a loving heart s'so true

Oh, Mother Sw…scratcher

We give our s'souls to you."

The War Begins

As Truth and Intelligence Chief, Whistle's job was to find out stuff. She' recently spied that Seward would leave the Palace in the evening to visit a patch of land near the river. Further spying revealed that the patch of land belonged to a water vole, Whistle was unsure, but thought it was Maj the Water Vole. After tea that evening, Whistle and Scratcher left Tip Top Turkey Trot and found themselves a tall rock to perch and observe. Sure enough, just as the sun was getting ready for bedtime, there was movement at the entrance of the Palace. Cindy's large frame came into view, she was carrying Seward. With a casual wave to the guards on the gate, they headed off in the direction of the vole's home.

Scratcher and Whistle followed, arriving at the water voles burrow just in time to see Seward disappear inside.

"Shhh, shhh!" whispered Scratcher.

From the vole's burrow they could hear the sound of voices, a muffled conversation and some laughter, but no matter how hard they listened, neither Scratcher nor Whistle could clearly hear what was being said.

In truth, Maj the Water Vole was a renowned knitter, and after the loss of Norris and to cheer herself up, Seward had commissioned Maj to make her a new hat. This was simply one of the fittings.

In no time at all, Seward re-emerged from the den. Once safely on Cindy's back, she waved goodbye to Maj and they returned to the Palace.

Confused, Scratcher glared at her daughter, "We need to find out what that was all about."

Like a couple of commandos, they scuttled forward towards Maj's burrow.

After a quick sniff at the entrance, Scratcher tapped the front door, put on her best smile, then politely stepped back and waited…. and waited. With no response, she knocked again. With still no reply she knocked a third time and began stomping back and forth.

"Drag her out," Whistle whistled.

In Scratcher's book not answering the door to a guest was the height of bad manners. She wasn't going to try a fourth time, so taking her daughters advise she began digging. In no time at all she had hold of the little critter in her beak. On seeing Maj exposed, Whistle joined her mother, then began a tug of war with Maj squealing as she was pulled and stretched. Finally Whistle let go and Scratcher ran off with the vole in her beak towards the river. There Scratcher pinned Maj down with her large gnarly foot.

Whistle began the questioning with a sharp peck on the vole's ear, then the other one, a softening-up process.

Scratcher grinned sarcastically, "That's no way to treat a friend."

After landing a particularly painful peck to Maj's tail, Whistle chuckled in her distinctive whistle, "So ss'orry, did I hurt you?"

At that Maj sank her teeth into Scratcher's foot making her jump into the air. The vole saw its chance and before you knew it, she'd slipped past Whistle and scrambled into the centre of a thick clump of reeds on the rivers edge.

With each blaming the other for the vole's escape, the turkeys began to search. They poked, scratched and stamped at the clump, but little Maj held her nerve.

A friendly cricket in the thicket had noticed the commotion and decided to help Maj by chirping for all it was worth to drown out any sounds of her movement.

"All's I can hear's is's kw'ickets," said Whistle, trotting back and forth between the reeds.

"We'll find it. I'll be damned if we don't," replied Scratcher.

But despite the ruckus surrounding her, Maj stayed still and silent. Minutes and maybe even hours passed and slowly the gobbles faded. Perhaps they were leaving thought Maj. But she was no fool, so stayed exactly where she was until the moon appeared, then snatched the cricket from its perch for a light supper and headed home.

The following morning there was the lightest tap on the Palace gates. Cindy looked down.

Standing there was Maj.

"Have you finished the hat?" asked Cindy.

"No," said Maj, and in an over-excited tone, she explained the previous days scenario, finishing with, "Why didn't they just eat me?"

Cindy thought for a moment. *She had a point; why hadn't the turkeys simply eaten her? Cats, yes, they were renowned for playing with their food, dogs occasionally, but turkeys never. The vole was right. It didn't add up.*

Taking a meerkat servant with her, Cindy went off to Tip Top Turkey Trot to investigate.

She was met at the entrance by Turvey, "What are you doing over here, big fella?" the tail of a worm hanging loosely from his beak. He glanced at the meerkat, winked and blew a kiss. "Cute."

"By order of the King, I demand to speak to your leader."

"You do now, do you," Turvey replied, "Well, she ain't here, so… talk to me."

"I need to speak to your leader."

Turvey spat out the remains of the worm and ground it into the soil with his foot. He glanced up and hissed, "Speak to me."

Cindy wasn't the sort to take any of this nonsense. With a swipe of her trunk, she roughly pushed Turvey to one side.

Suddenly, she was surrounded by dozens of angry, scratching, pecking turkeys. Some flew at her eyes, others ripped at her ears, and a whole lot more pecked at her rear end. Turvey had recovered and managed to grab hold of the tip of her tongue and was pulling with all his might. The pain was excruciating, Cindy could feel a panic attack coming on. She swung her head and swiped at him with her trunk, but no matter what Turvey held on. Turkeys were now everywhere, pecking, scratching and gouging at her private and un-private parts. Trumpeting in terror, Cindy turned on her heels and ran as fast as she could away from Tip Top Turkey Trot, only glancing back to see the turkeys swarming over the meerkat.

*

Cindy entered the King's Royal Quarters.

Seward was draped over her throne, idly chatting to Maj. "Maj tells me she was kidnapped by those awful turkeys."

"I have just returned from Tip Top Turkey Trot, Your Majesty," replied Cindy.

"Would you like a blueberry?" Seward said, offering Maj one, "They're delicious."

Maj leant forward, "Thank you, I will," positively drooling over the juicy fruits.

"And what exactly are we doing about it?" Seward fixed Cindy with an icy glare.

Cindy fumbled with her trunk, "Your Majesty, I've

been out there…. They've captured…." She knew it was far more than captured…. "One of the servants."

Seward shrugged nonchalantly, "How did that come about?"

For a moment Cindy lost her train of thought as, in the corner of her eye, she caught sight of Maj stuffing her cheeks with blueberries. Hoggery was one thing that Cindy deplored. She shook her head in disgust, then turned her attention back to the King. "Your Majesty. This can't go on. They're a law unto themselves."

"Another blueberry," offered Seward.

Preparing the Troops

Scratcher called a meeting. Things had come to a head;

"We have to prepare," she declared.

Scratcher gave instructions for Whistle to find out from the hairless apes how they made fire. "Threaten them if you need to," she added. Turvey was to spread the word around the Kingdom of Xum, that... Scratcher thought for a moment, "That the snail and the elephant have given birth to a monster... Yeah, a creature with the trunk and ears of an elephant, and the head and body of a snail." She chuckled at the thought.

"What about its's s'shell?" Whistle whistled.

"It ain't got one," Scratcher laughed.

Now, dear readers, I know what some of you are thinking. Outrageous, impossible; he's taking us for fools. Rest assured, I would not dream of taking my readers as fools. Far from it, so I will attempt to answer your question. The question is, if Cindy and Seward are both female, how could they possibly have a baby? Am I right? I refer you back to the start of the story when I explained that snails are in fact hermaphrodites, and can mate with either a male or female. So, there we go, perfectly possible.

*

It was already hot when Whistle set off. After hours and hours of travelling under the blazing sun, she flapped up into a daffodil tree to take a nap. It was from there she spotted them in a clearing. Whistle's opinion on hairless apes was that they are good for only two things, fighting and being lazy. This group were definitely veering towards the later. There were about fifty of them lounging in the sunshine, either scratching or making rude noises with their mouths and bottoms. Whistle's plan was to grab hold of their leader, work him or her over, and then come to some sort of deal in which Whistle would leave with the secret of fire. Her first job was identifying the leader. After about half an hour of watching, she decided it was the big fat one that all the other apes were fussing over. She was about to flap down and muscle in when away from the group she spotted a couple of their young playing with stones. Whistle smiled and licked her crooked beak; she was particularly fond of young hairless apes; they were almost as tasty as fresh piglets.

One of the baby apes had straight black hair, the other

curly white. They both were having great fun; jumping up and down, smashing the stones together. As she watched them play, something caught Whistle's eye. It was a spark. The black-haired baby bent close and began blowing, and soon the spark became a flame, and the flame turned into a fire.

*

Gossip is like strawberry jam; the juicier, the better it spreads, and the rumour about Seward and Cindy having a child together spread like wildfire. Harold and Berti, the unicorns, were so shocked and disgusted by the thought, that they left the Palace and were never seen again. But the story soon became the most talked about subject in the Kingdom. Of course, animals, such as lions, eagles, horses and dogs outwardly found such tittle-tattle vulgar and undignified, but in private everyone lapped it up.

Seward was outraged and called in her staff to find out where this disgusting rumour had started. All knew of it, but none knew its origin. A hen said she had heard it from a horse. The horse said it had come from a walrus and the walrus blamed it on a fish. But eventually, the source of the lie was tracked back to Tip Top Turkey Trot.

Seward felt her blood boil. Cindy was right; the turkeys had to be dealt with.

*

A lisping gobble rang out through the darkness. Moments later Whistle appeared at the entrance of Tip Top Turkey Trot.

Seeing the little apes tucked under her daughter's wings, Scratcher hopped down from her roost. "By my tail feathers, what have you got there?"

Whistle raised her wings and the small hairless apes tumbled to the ground.

In no time at all a crowd of squawking turkeys had gathered, sharp beaks testing the youngsters for their tenderness.

"No…. No…. No! Whistle, whistled, defending the pair, "These two hold the s'secret,". "We ain't got no fire without thes'sse. Get some s'stones."

Scratcher nodded and a young turkey dashed off, returning a moments later with a clutch of pebbles.

Whistle flung the stones down in front of the infants. "Watch this."

All eyes were fixed on the young apes, but neither showed the slightest interest in the surrounding rocks. Seconds passed, then minutes. Turkeys exchanged bewildered glances, then shifted their gaze to Whistle.

Whistle stomped between the two and grabbed hold of the stones with her big clawed feet, "They were doing thiss earlier," she clacked the stones together. "Come on," she said, encouragingly. "Jus'st clack them, like you did earlier…. Come on, come on," she gave the rocks another crack and to her astonishment, a spark flew. She clacked again, another spark, then another and another. Whistle now had a rhythm, with sparks flying every which way. Some landed on a pile of leftover feathers, and suddenly they had a blaze.

Scratcher grinned, "That's my girl."

*

Scratcher eyes went to a row of palm tree saplings that would serve as her anchor points, and meticulously measuring the distance from the entrance of Tip Top Turkey Trot, she chose her spot. Once satisfied with her calculations, she mixed some feathers and turkey poo into a ball and placed it into a V-shaped crevice on a flexible branch. Drawing back, she let fly… the initial attempt proved hopeless as the lightweight mix simply fluttered to her feet. Scratcher went to her favourite perch to ponder.

By morning an idea had surfaced, which proved to be a game-changer. What if she were to wrap the "flingers," Scratchers term for her bombs, around pebbles to give them a bit of purchase. It worked.

Soon she'd honed her skills and was able to launch the flingers and hit the target three times out of five. Whistle provided the spark, and it was all flingers blazing.

The Battle of Tip Top Turkey Trot

Scratcher ran through the drill, and once satisfied all knew their tasks, she selected a spot high in an oak tree for an overview and to gobble out her orders from.

Whistle was in charge of the young turkeys, the fire starters. It was on them to provide ammunition to the sharpshooters. The infantry was made up of eighty-one battle seasoned turkeys, all with sharpened poles. Their job was to push the enemy towards ambush central. Turvey had been appointed chief sharpshooter.

It was mid-morning when their scout returned with news that Cindy was leading a group of elephants, camels, hippos and gibbons; all armed and dangerous and heading their way. All went quiet in Tip Top Turkey Trot. Not a gobble nor a flutter of wings could be heard. Scratcher's troops were primed. Aerial squadron were in the trees. The infantry was in position, and Turvey and the sharpshooters were directly in line with ambush central.

Scratcher glanced down at Whistle.

Whistle saluted, then picked up her stones, she too was ready.

On the King's side, Cindy's plan was to trample and smash through the site using bulk, and if any turkeys got lippy, a well-aimed swipe of a trunk would make them see sense. Seward had made it clear that Tip Top Turkey Trot was to be levelled, using as much force as necessary.

There was movement; swaying branches, a rustle of leaves, birds fleeing.

A low rumble of elephant chitty chat could be heard, along with squeals, bleats and the occasional honk from the hippos. A fearful boar darted from the undergrowth, dashing this way and then that, before disappearing again.

Silence again.

Seward was sitting centre of Cindy's shoulders, a laurel leaf wrapped around her tender body and a hazelnut helmet on her head. She looked quite heroic waving her tiny banner.

Cindy raised her trunk and halted in her tracks; her ears flapped forward. *Something's wrong?* She tasted the air; it was unfamiliar. With her ears flapped forward she listened. *Turkey Trot was usually abuzz with gobbles and squabbles. It was too quiet;*

something was very wrong. No birdsong, no cricket chirps, no rustle of animals, nothing. "Your Majesty, this does not feel right."

Seward slithered forward, "What doesn't feel right?"

Cindy didn't respond; with her trunk in the air, she took a sniff to filtered the breeze.

"What's going on?" whispered one of the hippos.

Cindy glared back at the hippo. Her brain was whirling back in time trying to remember something. *This doesn't feel right at all, not one bit.* She took another step, then paused as her memory banks filtered, when a tap from Seward's flagpole brought her back to reality.

"Get on with it! We haven't got all day," grumbled Seward.

Scratcher was watching on, she was waiting to give the signal to attack, but wanted the enemy smack bang in the middle of ambush central. She looked to Whistle, held up her wing, and whispered a low-pitched gobble. Whistle got to work with her stones and had a fire going in no time. Keen young turkeys were already moving ammo to the sharpshooters. Unable to wait any longer Scratcher let out a low throaty noise, then dropped her left wing.

The aerial division launched a volley of flingers.

As the flaming flingers flew overhead, Cindy looked up, her mind clicking through slow cogs. Occasionally she'd seen a shooting star, but never so many?

Along with the camels, hippos, and gibbons, Seward too was dumbfounded and hypnotised by the flaming stars. Even when the burning feathers landed on the backs of the animals, they stood motionless.

The infantry began moved forward, their sharpened poles stabbing into the soft backsides of the hippos, who blindly charged forward, barging past camels and trampling over the gibbons. Unfortunately, the hippos ran straight into the sharpshooters' line of fire.

Cindy's trumpet blast, splashed through the silence like a frog in a puddle. *What was happening could only mean one thing. The sky was falling in.* With her tail and ears ablaze she forgot her mission, the turkeys and even her King.

It was carnage. Elephants trumpeting, camels grunting, gibbons screaming, and hippos honking. Scratcher leapt onto Cindy's back. Seward's eyes widened, ablaze with ignorance and fear. One swipe from Scratcher's claw sent the King's helmet flying.

"Call yourself a King?" another swipe knocked

Seward clean out of her shell and onto the ground, her body bare and exposed. Scratcher leapt down and snatched up the helpless Seward in her beak. Whistle had joined her mother, and like poor Maj the vole, Seward was stretched like an elastic band in their brutal game of tug of war.

The pain was excruciating, Seward saw the sky flash by, flames, then Cindy's legs and trunk. A gibbon's terrified face came into view and was gone again. The last thing she remembered was being hurled to the ground; sure she was dead.

*

Only three elephants, two hippos and a single gibbon made it out alive. None of the camels survived. Cindy's eyes were black with sooty tears, her trunk and feet were burnt and covered in blisters. The campaign had been a total disaster.

As they trundled back towards the Palace, one of the elephants asked what had become of Seward? No one seemed to know. A hippo though she'd been taken prisoner. The surviving gibbon chipped in saying he saw one of the turkeys kill and eat her. Cindy didn't comment, in her mind once more she had failed her King. About a mile from the Palace, they stopped at a water pool to cool down and bath their wounds. As her friends licked their wounds at the edge of the water, Cindy went to the far side and submerged herself. She had made up her mind to end it all, and deeper into the murky darkness she went. As her life ebbed from consciousness to oblivion, she felt something tickling inside her trunk, it was infuriating. *Would nothing go right?* She had to resurfaced and when she did, she let out a huge sneeze, and to everyone's surprise and delight, she dislodged Seward from inside.

*

That night, in Tip Top Turkey Trot, they celebrated a great victory. None of the turkey's had died and very few were injured.

Scratcher snatched up the corpse of a gibbon in her beak. "Feast tonight my friends," then opened up her throat and swallowed it down in one.

A huge cheer rang out.

Tickle & Pickle

Whistle was in love; the subject of her passion were the young apes. On waking, she'd get the two of them down from their nighttime perch for a wash, then she'd feed them helpings of eggs, and once breakfast was over, it was playtime. They made her laugh and at times cry, but filled her heart with joy. The blond boy, she called Tickle. He was a bit of a rascal and hung out with a gang of young turkeys called the Tick Tock Tigers. The little girl, she'd named Pickle, who loved nothing better than tucking herself up under her adopted mother's wing. Whistle protected them and as they grew taught them the ways of the world. Things such as, kill first and ask questions later. Always compliment your foe, once you've conquered them. Or even, four and four makes forty-four, or any number you like, as there's no such thing as the truth, only what you want to believe.

*

To get the blood moving and help keep herself in shape, Scratcher would take a vigorous morning walk around Tip Top Turkey Trot. She'd do ten minutes of running on the spot, some stretches and then finish off with high kicks. On this particular day her walk took her to an overgrown patch of woodland. She was about to head home when the distinct smell of rotting flesh wafted over her beak. After a bit of poking and sniffing, her nose led her to an old oak tree. Tucked under its bough the carcase of a small turkey.

Everyday cannibalism was strictly forbidden in the Tip Top Turkey Trot. The only exception being on the death of a hero when the body was consumed, allowing the hero's essence to enter the flock.

Scratcher bent down to look at the remains, which looked as if they had been roasted.

Whistle? No, it couldn't be. Pickle Probably not. No, it'll be her brother, that brat Tickle. Picking up the carcass she set off. A loud gobble and a sharp swipe of her beak got Tickle's attention, "Did you kill that chick?" Scratcher asked, throwing down the carcass.

Tickle looked to Whistle for reassurance, then to Scratcher, "I didn't do anything; it killed itself, I had to eat it. It was self-defence."

"And roasted itself, too," Scratcher directed a sharp peck to the side of Tickle's head, and before he had a chance to rub it, she'd delivered another peck to the other side.

Whistle called out, "He's only young. I'm s'sure he

didn't mean it."

Scratcher rained down peck after peck, Tickle was yelping, screaming and crying. He tried running away, his little legs scrambling, but Scratcher held him fast.

"You'll take that, and that," Scratcher gobbled as she climbed on top of Tickle, claws gouging, ripping.

Whistle tried to intervene but was roughly pushed away.

Suddenly Scratcher stopped, one last scratch left a scar on the young ape's face. "Death next time! You hear me!" She turned to Whistle, "You know the law, now you owe me. From now on he's mine; remember that." Scratcher turned her anger on Pickle, "You too."

In truth, Scratcher didn't give two figs about a young turkey getting eaten, she'd often gobbled one down herself if no one was around. Rules were there to be broken was her philosophy. No, there was another reason why Scratcher disliked the infant apes, that being, the amount of time Whistle was spending with them. Gone were the days when she and Whistle would go out hunting together. There was no more plotting the downfall of the snail, or even cosy evenings watching the sun go down. All her daughter was interested in these days were those two blasted apes.

The Truce

It was a chilly morning when five hundred turkeys led by Turvey and Whistle left Tip Top Turkey Trot. As soon as the Palace guards spotted the mob approaching, a trumpet sounded. The drawbridge dropped, and a hundred or more black-as-night buffalos charged out, creating a defensive semi-circle around the entrance.

Seward had called on the heavyweight mercenaries, sure the buffalo would teach the troublesome turkeys a final lesson.

*

Scratcher had positioned herself on a large termite mound a little distant from the action. From there she could look out over and command her troops. Turvey and his sharpshooters began moving towards the buffalo. Behind him was Whistle and a phalanx of three hundred turkeys, all with sharpened poles smeared with turkey poop which had been allowed to fester.

The lead buffalo shook his head, pawed the ground and threw dust over himself. The rest of the herd followed suit, impatient for battle. The buffalos charged, Turvey troops were first to meet them, launching volley after volley of flaming flingers at the bad-tempered bovines. The initial brave actions of the horned beasts quickly dissipated as they soon turned tail and ran back towards their lines.

"All grunt but no feathers," Turvey laughed, and with a wave of his wing commanded the sharpshooters forward.

The buffalo reassembled forming a defensive wall of flesh directly in front of the Palace entrance. With their murderous horns facing out it looked like a stalemate.

If he could bring down the heavy drawbridge, Turvey thought, then wham bam, as sure as eggs is eggs, Whistle and her troops would do the rest. Like a fire storm in the sky, flinger after flinger flew, and with Turvey's final shot he hit the drawbridge support rope. It was only a matter of time. Pushing forward he began taking the battle to the enemy, pushing the buffalo into a tighter and tighter spot. Suddenly there was an almighty crack, the buffalo scattered, and with a thud the drawbridge crashed to the ground trapping the unfortunate Turvey and the bravest of his band beneath it.

Whistle had no idea of her brother's demise, as she

and the infantry were busy jabbing the fleeing buffalo. But whilst Whistle was ignorant to her brother's plight, a stunned Scratcher had seen it all. Confused, she couldn't quite digest what she had just witnessed. *Perhaps he's ok? He'll be fine.* But from her heart came the pain, the pain that told her that she would never see her son alive again. "Be brave," she mumbled to herself, "Be brave. This is the price we pay." A tear crept down her scaly cheek, "War is cruel, war is bitter." The crown was hers for the taking. But the thought of the buffalo trampling over his beautiful body was too much. She gobbled the retreat.

Scratcher needed to be alone, alone with her heart and her memories. She prayed to her mother Tyrra, she prayed to dead son Turvey, but neither answered. So, she prayed for vengeance, and in her heart, vengeance answered her.

The following morning, word arrived via a skunk that Scratcher could collect the remains of Turvey. She sent out a dozen pallbearers to collect his remains. Once back at Tip Top Turkey Trot, his mangled remains were laid out on a bed of eggshells. Scratcher sat vigil, as throughout the day, turkey after turkey passed by their hero to pay their last respects, and as the clock struck midnight, they ate him.

*

Accompanied by Whistle, Tickle and Pickle, Scratcher set off for the Palace. In front was Tickle waving a white flag, they were on their way to negotiate terms.

Cindy blocked their entrance, "You are not welcome," she snapped.

Whistle stepped forward, "We come in peace."

Cindy looked down at Scratcher and asked, "What sort of peace?"

Scratcher stared fiercely ahead; she had no intention of speaking to the elephant. In reality her plan was to get inside the Palace to assess the King's resolve, terms be damned.

The cheek, thought Cindy. But she was wise enough to know that all disputes need a settlement, so leaving them, she went to report to Seward.

The mere mention of turkeys terrified Seward, she shrunk back into her shell.

"We should hear what they have to say, Your Majesty."

"But what if they set fire to me again?" Seward peeked out. She looked weary and aged.

It was a possibility, Cindy thought. But Turvey was dead and there were no sharpshooter in sight. "I will position guards throughout," she told the King. "I can assure you that you will not be harmed, Your Majesty."

Scratcher, Whistle, Tickle and Pickle followed Cindy through the courtyard, past the stream, and the cactus maze, before arriving outside the Royal quarters. The guards checked the turkeys for weapons.

As Whistle was chatting with one of the elephants, Scratcher began scanning the walls and spotted a vine which led up to a window. *If that window is the King's room, it will be easy.* Her eyes flashed at Pickle, and then the vine.

In a flash, Pickle had already scrambled halfway up.

"Keep them under control," said the guard pulling him down.

*

Whistle bowed, "Thank you for allowing us an audience, Your Majesty... May my mother speak?"

Seward ignored the request, "What are they?" she asked of Tickle and Pickle tucked under Whistle's wing.

"They're mine," Whistle whistled defensively, "I found them. They're mine!"

Seward smiled, then turned her attention to Scratcher, "Address your King."

"I am glad to see you in good health, Your Majesty." Scratcher bowed and coughed out a sorrowful gobble before going on. "I apologise for any distress that you may have endured," again she bowed. "This… this quarrel has caused loss and heartache on both sides." Scratcher sniffed a tear away, took a moment to compose herself and went on, "I assure you it was not our intention to cause any harm, particularly to you, Your Majesty. The issues that have caused so much grief arose from a misunderstanding," she glanced at Cindy.

Cindy leant over and whispered something in Seward's ear but was waved away.

Scratcher waited…, then looked Seward directly in the eye, "I hope Your Majesty is willing to openly discuss matters which have given rise to this terrible violence…. If I can speak candidly?"

Seward nodded.

Scratcher made a sound, something between a cluck and a gobble, "I don't want to be audacious," she glanced again at Cindy. "But I feel that the King is being improperly advised…. Sadly, from the beginning of time, turkeys have suffered persecution…." Her head dropped dolefully to one side and her wings spread to emphasise her point, "I don't know why this has happened; we have always tried to get along with our neighbours. I believe this matter could be resolved very easily." Scratcher's tone changed, her delivery was now strident, aggressive, bordering on intimidation, "Agree to an alliance and you can be assured of our loyal support." Another bow.

Seward hesitated before speaking, "What is it you are suggesting?"

Imploringly, Scratcher went on, "All we ask is a small piece of land…. a small piece, a section, a run, where we can live safely and unhindered. If you could give your blessing….?"

Seward smiled, she knew that a small piece would stretch into a medium section, then a medium piece into a large section, then a large piece until the turkeys had the whole Kingdom. But what was she to do? As sure as shells is shells, if she didn't agree, Scratcher and her rag tag army of turkeys would march on the Palace. Maybe Cindy could defend it, but then again, maybe not. No, she couldn't rely on Cindy.

Like naughty children often do at serious occasions, Tickle and Pickle began squabbling, Whistle pulled them away, "They're still young, Your Majesty. Please forgive them," she offered apologetically.

Seward tilted her head over to one side and watched the mischievous infants for a few moments, "Yes, we were all young once."

Scratcher gave the two a scolding glance, which soon put an end to Tickle and Pickle's fun.

"Let me consider," said Seward.

Scratcher's smile arrived just in time, "As you wish, Your Majesty." Bowing she turned, and nodded at Whistle.

*

As Scratcher was on her morning walk a message arrived requesting that she attend a meeting with the King, unescorted. She didn't trust the snail, so, before leaving, Scratcher issued instructions, that if she failed to return by nightfall, Whistle was to rally the troops and storm the Palace.

Scratcher was met by Cindy and led through to the King.

"After considering yesterday's meeting, I believe we

can agree on terms," said Seward. "But, for the dispute to settle, it requires compromise by both parties. So yes, you can have a separate area from the Kingdom, which I will fully sanction and endorse. I only ask for you to pledge loyalty and sign a declaration of peace before your King and the nobles of the Kingdom of … and for your daughter to live at the Palace as our guest. A token of your goodwill."

Scratcher hadn't expected this. The snail had outflanked her. With a hesitant stutter, "Tha…t's very gracious…. Your offer is very reasonable, Your Majesty. For my part I agree and by my honour pledge my full and unreserved loyalty to you, Your Majesty. I'm sure Whistle will be delighted to join you at the Palace."

As she made her way back to Tip Top Turkey Trot. Scratcher thought over the idea. *It could work to their advantage. Whistle would undoubtedly kick up a stink, but when gobble came to peck, she'd do as her mother told her.*

Arriving home, she went through the option with Whistle.

"No, no, no!" was Whistle's reply.

"But it's a golden opportunity."

"No, no, no," continued Whistle, "I'm not leaving my

babies for anyone, or anything," glancing at Tickle and Pickle.

Scratcher paced back and forth, occasionally looking back at the two youngsters. Finally, she scratched the floor twice, and to seal the deal pushed forward her wing. "Ok, I'll make sure those two go with you?"

But Whistle was still reluctant.

"Come on, meet me halfway," said Scratcher, her wing jutting further forward, "Halfway."

Whistle feared her mother, she knew to defy her would mean consequences.

Scratcher interrupted her train of thought, "Think about it; but I must know by the morning." With a brusque flap of her wings Scratcher took to the air and left.

When Whistle explained the situation to Tickle and Pickle, they burst into tears. Neither wanted to leave Tip Top Turkey Trot and go to live in the Palace.

"You are both getting big. It will be a great adventure. An introduction to polite society."

"I don't want to be polite society. I want to stay here," cried Tickle, huffing as he stamped his foot.

"Nor me!" screamed Pickle.

"Well, it's not certain anyway. Mother S'scratcher will ask the King if you can come with me."

"So, you'll go anyway?" asked Pickle, her face a picture of anger and distress.

With a resigned nod of her head, "I have no choice."

Tickle and Pickle burst into noisy tears.

*

Seward was very happy to agree to Tickle and Pickle accompanying Whistle. In fact, having heard a lot about the ingenuity of the hairless ape species, and was intrigued to know more.

Whistle, Tickle and Pickle waved goodbye to Scratcher and all at Tip Top Turkey Trot and headed off to the Royal Palace. They were greeted by Cindy. The elephant led them through numerous corridors to a suite of rooms that would be their quarters. It was far more luxurious than anything Whistle had experienced before. The bedding was soft, the decorations beautiful, and they even had a private garden. Tickle and Pickle's initial reluctance quickly gave way to curiosity and excitement as they explored their new surroundings.

A gala dinner to celebrate the truce was arranged. A total of two thousand and fifteen guests were invited. Servants had been dashing around all week in preparation. The grand dining hall was set out with three long lines of tables. Guests were seated by meritocracy with dignitaries and nobles seated closest to the King. Poor Wally the Warthog nearest the door. The King and a small entourage were sat on a smaller table at the front. Scratcher was not a one for fancy dinners and gentile conversation, so she excused herself saying she was suffering a dose of turkey flu, but said that her daughter would represent her. To honour Whistle's presence, she was seated alongside Seward.

The starter of seaweed and brown algae was served.

Not all the guests were impressed, "Very tasty," said Whistle lying, "What do you call this?"

With pangs of longing, Seward recalled her first encounter with the fruits of the sea. But her thoughts of Norris were interrupted.

"Would you ever consider moving the Palace?" asked Whistle.

Seward gave her a look of distain.

Whistle was not put off however, "It's a very big place to keep tidy…."

Seward was regretting having the turkey alongside her. With every answer came another question.

What do you think of your staff? Cindy? Any room for improvement?" Questions, questions, questions. "What is your greatest strength and what is your greatest weakness?"

Seward's answers were vague. Which might sound like she was being guarded and diplomatic, but in truth she didn't really know or care.

The main course arrived; crushed spinach, with a side of lettuce and a drizzle of nettle jus.

Whistle put aside her disgust and ate with gusto and even complimented the food. Whistle had now moved on the conversation and was babbling on about spirituality and the meaning of life.

Thankfully for Seward, Cindy interrupted. "Your Majesty, the porcupine joust is about to start. Would you like for me to move you to your throne?"

Oh yes please."

*

As befitted her job of Chief of Truth and Intelligence, Whistle began observing routines and soon became familiar with the comings and goings of the Palace.

At any gathering or meeting, she'd be there encouraging all to share their concerns. Some moaned about Cindy's bathing habit of leaving a mess in the drinking water. Hippos complained that all the elephant guards were bullies, and Cindy was the worst of them. The servants were more concerned with the King's pompous attitude, and her reluctance to make decisions, even quite trivial ones, "One of the worst kings we've ever had," said Sammy the Squirrel. In fact, it was hard to get a positive response about life at the Palace from anyone. All grist to the mill as far as Whistle was concerned.

Crikey

Back in Tip Top Turkey Trot, Scratcher had been updating the place. First on her to do list had been a new fence, which took the turkeys eight months to complete. Unfortunately, no sooner was it finished than a boar smashed through and stole some eggs. Scratcher had the boar tracked down and needless to say the boar paid a lot more for the eggs than they were worth. To prevent a repeat, she then decided to build a solid wall of pebbles and stones, with fortifications, lookout posts, and a drawbridge. In all respects, it was a poor man's version of the Palace.

*

Despite her initial reluctance, Whistle was enjoying her time at the Palace, life was good. Here she had her pick of beautiful clothes, all she could eat, as well as private rooms for herself and Tickle and Pickle. The two ape children had in fact become firm Royal favourites. Seward, like Whistle had become entranced by the joy they provided and loved to watch them play. Pickle invented a Whirly Gig, a kind of primitive wheel, which she hit with a stick and chased. Tickle had a Spinner, a stone on a piece of string that he loved swinging around and around. They played games, like fling the frog, and choke the cat. Swing the Snake became so popular that even to this day snakes are very wary of hairless apes. No, for Whistle, the move had proved a great success. So for now she hid the file she had on Cindy.

However Scratcher was getting impatient. She'd only received a smattering of notes from her Truth and Intelligent Chief, and they were all about what a good life they were having. There was no mention of the King's routine or even when the guards went to bed. Her daughter seemed to have forgotten the reason for her stay. Scratcher sent a message via a dickie bird saying that in three days, she would arrive at the Palace disguised as a beggar, and it would be up to Whistle to bust her in.

With a knobbly walking stick stuck under her wing as support, and a mess of grey mud and cranberry juice smeared over her feathers, Scratcher arrived at the Palace gates, "Alms, alms... Alms for a beggar," she called out.

The spy hole slid open. A dewy eye peered out, and bolts were slid back. An elephant guard emerged, took a couple of sniffs and gruffly asked, "What do you want?"

"Alms, alms, for a weary traveller," Scratcher replied, reaching out a pitiful wing.

Slamming the door closed, the elephant disappeared

inside. Scratcher tilted an ear; she hearing the elephant's heavy footsteps faded into the distance. Up on the battlements two of the gibbons were idly chatting. One, a stringy fellow with dark rings around his eyes stared challengingly down at Scratcher.

She smiled sweetly. Out went her wing, "Alms, alms, alms for a beggar."

The gibbon screeched, reached behind itself and threw something disgusting in Scratcher's direction.

With the sound of a bolt being slid back, the gates swung open.

Whistle stepped forward, she was holding a basket of bread and a bowl of water, "Alms and refreshment for you, dear lowly beggar," and glancing at the guard, "I'll be fine. You may leave us."

The guard's trunk dipped into the bread basket and helped himself to a large piece of bread, then disappeared inside. Scratcher's eyes motioned to the gibbon, letting Whistle know they were being watched.

"Thank you, kind Miss," said Scratcher, coughing and pretending to stumble. "My dear, I have travelled for many days and nights; my body is tired. Is there somewhere where a beggar could lie down?"

Whistle raised her voice so the gibbon could hear, "I am sure the King will accommodate you." She pecked at the Palace gates; the guard pulled them open, "Do we have somewhere where this weary soul could rest?"

The elephant seemed non-plussed, his trunk went to his head, "Err, the compound…. maybe?"

"The compound?" Whistle whistled indignantly, "Where is your charity? The King will hear about this."

The elephant looked suitably chastised, "Erm…."

Whistle shook her head dismissively, "I will use my quarters," Another shake of her head, "The compound!" She looked to her mother, "Follow me," as they marched into the Palace.

Scratcher didn't say a word as she wandered around Whistle's quarters. She picked up a silk robe and sniffed it. A sniggering smile appeared on her face.

Knowing her mother's thoughts, "It wasn't my idea, remember," said Whistle.

Scratcher shook her wattle head back and forth, "No, it wasn't."

There was a loud bang, then a crash as Tickle came

blustering in. At the sight of Scratcher, he stopped dead. His happy face turned to fear. Tickle was taller now, but thin and gangly, with black hair hanging down over his shoulders.

"Come to granny, child."

Tickle's lip quivered.

"Come, come."

Tickle let out a mix-up of a grunt and a squeal, turned on his heels and was gone.

"Stop him!" Scratcher screeched.

"Don't worry, he's been drilled."

"He'd better be," said Scratcher glaring at her daughter,

"Sit." said Whistle, pushing a stool forward. "He's fine. He won't say a word."

Scratcher sat down, she raised her feet and chuckled, "Fooled them, didn't I." Proud of her disguise she let out a fruity gobble.

Whistle reached under her bed and pulled out a slate and slid it across the floor, "Have a look." It was her file on Seward and Cindy.

To the average reader it was nothing more than a mess of turkey footprints, but Scratcher quickly deciphered the marks.

"Good work... But!" her tone was changed, "Enough of what the squirrel and the hippos think. Tell me what you know about the snail?"

"What is there to tell? The King wakes early, takes breakfasts, walks the grounds then takes lunch. She has a bath and a massage in the afternoon, naps and is never seen in the evening."

"Never seen in the evening! Where does she go in the evening?

"I don't know."

Scratcher scratched the floor in frustration, then wandered over to the window, "Nice life you've got here. Yes. Very nice indeed." She picked up a juicy pear off the ledge and took a bite before turning to face her daughter, "I hope you haven't forgotten why you are here?"

Whistle looked vacant.

"What is your title?" snapped Scratcher.

"What!"

"Your title! What is it?"

Whistle's mumbled "Chief of Truth and Intelligence."

"Yes, Chief of Truth and Intelligence!" Scratcher gobbled out. "And what part of that job do you not understand?" she waited, "Because if you are Chief of Truth and Intelligence, why have I not had any truth or intelligence from you?" She picked up the slate, her voice was edgy, threatening, "This…. This is all you have after all this time." Suddenly Scratcher's eyes flicked past her daughter.

Pickle entered the room. "Hello Granny. We've been so much looking forward to your visit and have got so much to tell, haven't we mummy? My word, I didn't recognise you."

Scratcher laughed and opened her wings wide, "Come here, sweetheart,"

Pickle dashed forward.

"Haven't you grown?" said Scratcher, looking Pickle up and down. "Beautiful, beautiful. Isn't she beautiful? Takes after her old Granny."

Pickle had indeed grown, and maybe to a turkey she would be described as beautiful. Her eyes had narrowed, her nose and neck had lengthened, and she'd developed a stoop. "Tell me everything that's been going on in Turkey Trot Granny?" Pickle attitude was charming, confident, and devious.

"Oh, you wouldn't recognise the place. We now have walls with lookout towers. I'm even thinking about a moat. No one in or out without my permission," Scratcher winked.

Pickle glanced over her shoulder, "A moat mummy, Granny digging a moat."

Whistle smiled.

"And inside The Trot? What's changed?" asked Pickle.

Scratcher's head tilted over to one side, then the other, as she mulled over question, "Why, nothing."

"Nothing, mummy," Pickle glanced back again. "Of course, silly me, it's perfect. Why would you change it?"

Whistle nodded gracefully, "Yes, why would you?"

"We've missed you so much granny. Haven't we, mummy?"

Scratcher seemed utterly taken in by Pickles' flattery. "Enough about me. Tell me everything that has happened since you have been here."

Pickle took a deep breath before regaling how poorly they had been treated. Every day they were made to march up and down in front of the stupid King, which no one liked. She said the rest of the animals were only at the Palace on sufferance, and as soon as Scratcher could organise an uprising, Pickle was sure the other animals would get behind it.

"I always said Pickle would go far," said Scratcher. "The other one… 'Trickle', well…. I'm not so sure.

"It's Tickle Granny, Tickle, not Trickle," said Pickle.

"It'll be trickle soon enough," chuckled Scratcher.

Whistle stood back, proud of how well Pickle had handled herself and the situation. She could not remember teaching her the skills of persuasion, but without a doubt, Pickle was a natural.

"Right," said Scratcher, "I now have fifteen hundred turkeys willing to lay down their lives for our cause. We will attack next Tuesday week, first thing in the morning." For some reason she checked her wing, then fixed Whistle with her beady eye, "All I need you to do is to knock out the guards on the gate and then pull it open. Then lay down a line of breadcrumbs all the way to the snail's quarters."

Whistle thought there was no chance of her shifting the gates alone or knocking out the elephant on duty, never mind the breadcrumbs. But regardless she nodded.

"Can you get me up into the snail's quarters?" Scratcher glanced at Pickle.

"Easy peasy," Pickle replied enthusiastically. But a moment later, "Hold on, Tuesday mornings, the King is in her counting house, counting out her strawberries.... What about Wednesday? Could you make it a Wednesday?"

Scratcher let out an angry gobble as her wattle blazed red. "So, where is the counting house? I'll squash her there."

"No can do!" said Pickle, "Not unless you can squeeze into a hole this big?" Pickle held up her fist and made a little hollow.

"The counting house is only that big?"

"Yeah, maybe even smaller," said Pickle squeezing her fist even tighter.

"So how many strawberries does the snail count in there?"

"There's only ever one, but it takes her all morning to count it."

Scratcher let out a ripple of gobbles in disgust.

The door creaked; the gormless face of Tickle peered into the room.

"Hey, Tweedle Dee, have you been listening?" asked Scratcher.

Tickle stood still.

"Well, come in. There are no prizes for staying at the back of the room," said Scratcher.

Tickle skulked forward and sat close to Whistle.

Scratcher shook her head wondering what had happened to him? She remembered back to the day he killed and cooked the turkey chick. *He was such a menace. He certainly had promise then. But something had changed. Why so lily-livered?*

Under Tickle's arm was a length of sapling with a string stretched from end to end, a bow of sorts. As the others looked on, he quietly placed it in his lap and began plucking. Plink plink, plunk plunk, plink, plunk. It was a dreadful tune but Scratcher was fascinated, her head dipping to the rhythm as she tried to figure out where the sound was coming from. When he'd finished, she stepped up and sniffed Tickle, he plucked the string once more; plink!

Scratcher jumped back.

"It's Tickle's squeaker," Pickle chuckled, "He's always playing with it."

Scratcher hopped forward again, sniffing the squeaker. "What is it?

"His squeaker," Whistle explained. "Tickle invented it. He makes all kind of things."

Scratcher nodded with surprise and pride, "Well, well, well, perhaps there's more to you than meets the eye."

Tickle blushed and began plucking once again.

Scratcher was back to the matter at hand. "So, Whistle, you'll knock out the guards and open the gate. I'll provide the feathers, honey, and hotdogs. And you, Pickle…."

"Breadcrumbs, honey …?" Whistle interrupted.

Scratcher grinned. "My dear, the power of confusion, distraction, and the three senses. Feathers to touch, honey to taste, and hotdogs to fight over?"

Whistle was still confused but knew better than to question her mother. Glancing at her son, "What about Tickle? What can he do?"

Scratcher patted Tickle's head. "And... you, Tickle, will have the most important job of all. You will stay here playing with your squeaker, won't you? We need someone to monitor things, gather information, and ensure our plans aren't discovered. You're our little spy in the Palace."

Tickle smiled mischievously; he liked the idea of being the quiet force behind their operation.

Let the Battle Commence

You often hear how small events dictate the outcome, and if it wasn't for a pesky bug, this war might never have got started.

It was Tuesday morning, the day before Wednesday morning. The barometer was hitting red hot and sweaty. Whistle was in her quarters nibbling her claws, worrying about the events due to unfold the following day. Pickle was enjoyed a lazy breakfast and Tickle was up on the battlements sunbathing.

As he was enjoying the early morning sunshine, a bug decided to join Tickle and took a particular liking to his nose. Giving the blighter a sharp flick sending the bug flying, Tickle thought that was the end of it. But for the bug, it was only the beginning. It returned with a vengeance, buzzing, circling, divebombing, anything to get at Tickle. Swat after swat, but the bug wasn't giving up. Finally, Tickle stood up, ready to take on the pesky nuisance.

It was then he spotted the hordes in the distance. It was as though Scratcher had completely forgotten the conversation with Pickle about the King being in the counting house Tuesday.

The guard on duty was new to the job. She was marching back and forth in front of the gates, and to keep herself company she sang out a song.

Dum dum, trumpity trump

When I'm on my beat

You better jump

Dum dum, trumpity trump,

If not, a slap

You'll get a thump

Dum dum, trumpity, trump…

"Hey, fatso," Tickle called out, ducking behind a dozing hippo.

The elephant turned abruptly, "Halt, who goes there?"

"Hey Fatso," Tickle ducked back out of sight.

"Who are you calling fatso?" said the guard giving the hippo a nudge with the sharp point of her tusk.

The hippo squealed and, in a flash, snapped its massive jaws down on the elephant's trunk. Of course this sent the elephant crazy, she wasn't going to take any nonsense from a hippo. And now we've got ourselves a fight.

Tickle slipped by the battling heavyweights, slid the bolt and swung open the gates.

The sight that befell him was breathtaking. The whole horizon was alive with turkeys, moving at incredible speed towards the Palace. They were in their war colours, blue feathers with bright black faces and green wattles. What was very strange though, was that there was no sound. The turkeys were on their tippytoes, not a squeak or a gobble from any of them. Scratcher was leading from the front, perched on the shoulders of a fearsome cock turkey.

Tickle dashed in on Whistle and his sister, "She's here, she's here."

Whistle jumped up, "Quick, quick, the Kings here!"

Pickle stood to attention and bowed, "Welcome, Your Majesty."

"Not the King, you nitwits. It's Granny! She here!"

Whistle and Pickle looked at each other in disbelief.

"You did say Wednesday, didn't you?" Whistle snapped.

Pickle had no time to respond as from outside came the shrill of a trumpet call. They all dashed to the window just in time to see the elephant guard struggle to close the gates. But she was to late the turkeys were already flooding in. With a swing of her trunk, the guard managed to flattened a section, but in her madness, she slipped and fell, the turkeys swarmed over her. From the shadows, the buffalos appeared and charged. Dust and turkeys flew as turkeys were tossed this way and that. The bovines were fighting bravely, but soon turkey after turkey became lodged on their curved horns until their mighty weapons were nothing more than feather dusters.

In a moment, Scratcher appeared. Her beady eye caught sight of Whistle, and with a click of her heels, the huge cock turkey leapt forward.

Cindy had rushed to the gates and was pushing with all her might hoping to get them closed, but with the weight of the turkeys pushing against her, she was making slow progress. A lion pounced on a group of the invaders, and in seconds they were nothing more than a pile of bloodied feathers. Giraffes charged into a thicket, their long legs flying off at all angles, but the turkeys were quick. Once behind their leggy opponents, the turkeys laid into the giraffe's tendons with sharpened beaks, peck after peck, until the giants fell.

"Where's the Snail?" Scratcher screamed, "Point me, point me!" her wings flapping in frustrated anger.

Without thinking, Tickle pointed to the counting-house.

With a squawk, Madame Ostrich stepped into the fray, her ungainly figure prancing here and there, "Pardon me, excuse me, Kings work, Kings work," squashing turkey after turkey under her huge feet.

"Where is she?" shouted Scratcher as she hopped off her steed, "Show me now."

Pickle turned and scampered forward. Following her, Scratcher, Whistle and Tickle pushed through a thicket of flesh until they reached the stairwell to the Royal quarters. Scratcher now took the lead, swiping a sharpened claw at any creature, friend or foe, who got in her way. They made their way step by step until they arrived at the King's rooms. Like a maniac, Scratcher tore at the bed of moss, but Seward was nowhere to be found.

"She'll be in the counting house," said Pickle.

Back down they went and then up through the Long Gallery.

Despite the furore outside, the royal artist hadn't noticed. Deep in concentration, the sloth had his paintbrush in the air and was very slowly bringing it down onto his canvas.

"Is the King here?" Scratcher aggressively gobbled.

The sloth finished his brushstroke, then very slowly looked up. "P…ardon."

Scratcher slashed at the poor creature's throat, then noticing the portraits of previous Kings and Queens, struck a pose, beak up, head to one side. The painting of Seward was on the Sloth's easel, Scratcher spat on it and knocked it to the floor. Then turning to the others, "Show me the way."

Crocodiles had now joined the guards and were beginning to hold the turkey marauders, but the battle wasn't over by a long chalk. Each side was now fighting over the bodies of fallen comrades, and with the ground soaked in blood, the fight was turning in favour of the more nibble footed. A particularly mean-looking turkey squared up to a meerkat. Like gladiators they hopped back and forth trying to get at each other, the turkey lashing out with its clawed feet, the meerkat with its paws, until a clumsy swipe from Cindy's trunk saw both turkey and meercat fly over the Palace wall. Meercats, squirrels, mice, ferrets, anything small and agile was now at the front, snapping, biting, nibbling at any loose turkey foot or wing, whilst the larger animals used their weight to hold back the masses.

They found Seward in the counting-house munching on a ripe strawberry. As they entered, she turned with a look of surprise. Then on spotting Whistle, she smiled; her eyelashes fluttered. She looked at the red shiny strawberry, "It's a beauty; would you like to try some?"

*

A blood-curdling gobble so full of hate and anger rang out, that it stopped the fighting in its tracks.

High on the battlements stood Scratcher, wings spread, and beak raised, the portrait of a demon. She slowly raised the pitiful body of King Seward, strawberry juice still dripping from her lips, and flung the tiny body down into the throng.

Long Live the King

I hope you all enjoyed this tale. A story in which we learnt that with strength and resilience the most unexpected individuals can surprise us. It's a reminder that greatness can come from anywhere, and even the smallest actions can have a profound impact on the world around us. Look beyond appearances and delve deeper to appreciate the potential within yourself and others.

A tale is never truly finished. It is always evolving, always growing, inviting us to explore new horizons of possibility. As we bid farewell to these characters who we have journeyed with through the highs and lows of their lives, let us carry their stories in our hearts.

May your own stories be filled with love, laughter, and endless possibilities.

Printed in Great Britain
by Amazon